Money
Matters

Ariennir yn Rhannol gan
Lywodraeth Cymru
Part Funded by
Welsh Government

Ariennir yn rhannol gan Lywodraeth Cymru fel rhan o'i
rhaglen gomisiynu adnoddau addysgu a dysgu Cymraeg
a dwyieithog

Part funded by the Welsh Government as part of its
Welsh and bilingual teaching and learning resources
commissioning programme

Turn out the light

by Manon Steffan Ros

illustrated by Rhiannon Sparks

Meg

Oh my goodness. It was the most ridiculous thing I'd ever seen. Jon's parents had always spoiled him terribly. He had every games console, every DVD and every game that had ever taken his fancy. He had his own laptop and a telly that almost covered an entire wall of his bedroom. He always had the latest iPad. And the worst thing was, Jon always made sure that everyone knew that he had more than the rest of us.

'What's that you've got? *Action Super Fight 2*?

Action Super Fight 3 is faaaar better … '

'Your football is okay. It's fine to use on the schoolyard. I don't want to bring my ball in – Mum says she doesn't want me to lose a ball that cost more than fifty quid!'

'I like your trainers. I used to have ones like that until Dad bought me a better pair.'

I'm making him sound terrible, aren't I? But Jon isn't a bad lad, really, just completely spoilt. Sometimes I pity him because he tries so hard to prove himself. He's just using all his expensive stuff to try and make people like him, and sometimes that works, for a while. It never lasts, though.

Jon was best friends with Sam, my twin, for a few months last year. He bought things for Sam every other day – sweets or chocolate, or sometimes even games or DVDs. Sam isn't the kind of person who likes confrontation, but I think he felt quite uncomfortable accepting all this stuff from Jon, and he soon went back to his old mates.

Anyway, Jon's birthday parties. They're awful. His parents always go overboard, and every year is worse than the last.

I'll give you some examples.

1. Jon's Eighth Birthday Party.
Jon's mother hired the cinema in town to show the new Spiderman film. There was a popcorn machine and pick-and-mix and pop, all free. Before and after the film, the screen showed photographs of Jon, taken over the course of his life. Eating pick&mix while looking at a photo of Jon as a toddler sitting on a potty was not a pleasant experience.

2. Jon's Ninth Birthday Party.

Jon's Dad hired a bus to take the whole class ice skating to somewhere near Rhyl. My best friend, Jess, fell and hurt her wrist, but Jon's parents weren't very sympathetic. While everyone else was in a restaurant scoffing burgers and chips, I was sitting with a crying Jess on the bus, trying to console her. It was not a pleasant experience. After we got home, Jess's parents took her to the hospital and found out that she'd fractured two bones in her wrist. She was in plaster for six weeks.

3. Jon's Tenth Birthday Party.

This one was truly awful. Jon's birthday is at the end of August, and so his parents made the mistake of thinking it was going to be sunny. That's what the weather forecast had said. They arranged a beach party, with a huge barbecue and a magician and a man who made sand sculptures. It was sunny for about half an hour, and then a huge storm broke: rumbling thunder, blinding lightning, the lot. The rain was terrible, like something from a film about the end of the world. Though the party moved to Jon's house, eating damp cake while freezing in wet shorts and a vest was not a pleasant experience.

And so it came to Jon's eleventh birthday party. Oh, my goodness. I'd half expected that I wouldn't be invited this year, but no, everyone in the class was given a huge invitation card with a cartoon drawing of Jon on the front. I could have stayed at home, I suppose, but I was curious after hearing Jon going on about it at school.

'Mum's spent *thousands* on this party. *Thousands,*'

he boasted one break time to whoever was close enough to hear. 'The food alone is costing over three hundred quid!'

I doubted that. Who spends three hundred pounds on food for a party? But once I arrived at the party, I realised that yes, he had been telling the truth.

It was ridiculous.

Jon's mother had hired a field at the edge of town, and there was a massive marquee, like the one they have for the Eisteddfod, but a bit smaller. Inside, there were lots of little tables with candles flickering on them, and photos of Jon everywhere. There was a DJ playing Jon's favourite songs, and disco lights were flashing. And the food! Posh stuff, like tiny burgers and miniscule hot dogs, and fruits I'd never heard of, and jars of sweets. In the centre of the marquee, there was a huge cake shaped like a volcano, with chocolate and sweets flowing from it instead of magma. Everyone had dressed up. (The invitations had specific instructions - *evening dress.)* Because the party was happening in the evening, the sparkling lights looked like stars.

'Wooooooooooow!' exclaimed Sam, my twin brother, as we arrived. It was already full, and everyone was laughing or dancing. Sam stared around, his mouth gaping.

'Yes, wow,' I agreed. 'Wow that he's having such a tacky party! Who does he think he is?'

Sam scowled. 'You're not seriously saying that you don't like all this?'

'I didn't say that,' I answered firmly. 'It's okay for a wedding, or for a party for someone celebrating their ... oh, I dunno ... eightieth? Hundredth?'

Sam decided to ignore me. 'Look at that cake! It actually looks like a volcano!'

'Yes, if volcanoes spewed pick-and-mix. But they don't.'

Oli, Sam's best friend, rushed over. 'Come and see these tiny burgers, Sam! We're having a competition to see who can fit most of them in their mouth at once.'

Thankfully, I'd seen Jess by then, so I barely saw Sam for the rest of the party.

'Can you believe this?' Jess asked, rolling her eyes. 'What a fuss just for an eleventh birthday!'

Thank goodness, I thought with a smile. Someone else who sees sense!

Sam

It was amazing!

Before we went home, everyone was ferried outside. I thought that was a bit odd. It was dark, and everything was so warm and cosy in the marquee. And then, the show started.

Fireworks.

They were incredible. They went on for five whole minutes with no breaks, filling the sky with colour. As people watched the sky, I looked at Jon, who was standing at the front. His parents stood behind him, hand in hand, and they were gazing at him with complete adoration. They were so glad that their boy had had such a successful party.

They must love him very much to spend that much money on him, I thought.

After the fireworks, everyone went back into the marquee to sing 'Happy Birthday to Jon' and to have some cake. It was delicious – I had a piece with a white chocolate mouse and a few malteasers in the icing. I'd stuffed my face all evening, and felt slightly sick, but it didn't matter.

Then we were each given a party bag, and people started to leave. I said goodbye to Oli and the others, and started walking home with my twin sister, Meg.

'Did you have a piece of cake?' I asked as we walked home. 'It was incredible.'

'It was okay.'

I shook my head. Meg was impossible to please. 'Oh, come on, Meg. That was a brilliant party.'

'If you like that kind of thing.'

Back at home, Mum was waiting for us. Though it was late, we stayed up and had some hot milk while we chatted about the party.

I emptied my party bag on the kitchen table.

'Goodness! A helicopter kit, a huge bar of chocolate, football stickers - and a bag of sweets!' I grinned. Jon's parents were so generous! 'What did you get, Meg?'

Meg upended her bag onto the table. She had the same as me, except that she had a different type of chocolate, and she had a set of nail varnishes instead of the helicopter kit.

'Wow!' Mum exclaimed. 'When I was a kid, party bags just had a piece of cake and a balloon.'

Meg pushed the nail varnish across the table. 'Here you go, Mum. I don't like nail varnish.'

Mum studied Meg's face. 'What's wrong, sweetheart? Didn't you have a good time?'

I sighed. 'She'd decided she was going to hate it before she even went to the party!'

'That's not true! I just think that it's a bit much for a birthday party, that's all. And now everyone else will think that their birthday parties aren't good enough, just because they don't have thousands of pounds to spend ... '

I hadn't thought about that.

'Are you worried about your birthday?' asked Mum, blowing the steam off her mug of hot milk.

Meg shrugged. 'I don't really care about parties. I just don't like it that Jon always shows off because he's rich.'

'Actually, I've been thinking about your birthdays. I know there's a while to go yet, but I thought that if we started saving up now, by that time we could take a trip to Oak Park adventure park!'

Meg and I loved that idea. Fair play to Mum. Things hadn't been easy for her since Dad had legged it, but she worked more shifts in the factory now, and she was obviously planning a special birthday for us. Never mind Jon's volcano cake and fireworks – Oak Park was miles better!

Mum and Meg and I sat up until late, chatting and giggling. I think we were as excited as each other about Oak Park, even Mum. She fetched the laptop and we browsed Oak Park's website, and saw all the rides.

'Even Jon will be jealous!' Meg grinned. 'I bet you he'll take the whole class to Oak Park on his twelfth birthday!' She was only joking, and I couldn't help giggling.

'And we'll travel there in limousines … ' I added.

'And his cake will be the size of Snowdon … ' said Mum.

'And the party bags will be huge, like binbags, and stuffed full of fifty-pound notes!'

As I lay in bed that night, I was truly happy. Usually, I worry about things late at night – things I don't have any control over, like war, and children dying of starvation, and why does Dad never phone. But for once, I felt okay. Perhaps Jon's parents had more money than us, and perhaps we'd never get a party like Jon had, but I was going to Oak Park on my birthday. Everyone in our house went to bed with a smile on their face that night.

I can remember that afternoon as if it happened yesterday.

Isn't it weird? Sometimes, when good things happen, I try to remember every detail – a joke, perhaps, or the taste of a particularly delicious birthday cake. But I always forget those kinds of things in time. Only the bad things tend to stick in my memory.

It was a normal afternoon in our house. It was over a fortnight since Jon's party. Meg was prickly (she always gets moody when she's hungry) and I was at the kitchen table, trying to finish my geography homework. Mum was making us both a sandwich, and the radio was blaring in the background. Mum loves the radio. That's the first thing she does when we get up in the morning, and when she gets in from work – she switches on the radio.

'Here you go,' said Mum, handing us a plate each – a jam sandwich for me, Marmite for Meg. Meg grabbed her sandwich and stuffed an entire half into her mouth at once.

'Thanks,' I said, ignoring the sandwich for now. The homework was difficult – I hated geography.

' ... And news just coming in,' said the man on the radio. 'It has been reported that the clothing factory, Crease, is to close. The work of making clothes for high-street stores will be transferred from Tywyn to an unspecified overseas location in order to save on costs ... '

It was as if someone had pressed the pause button on our family. My biro became still; Meg stopped chewing; Mum froze.

I was the first to speak.

'Mum?'

The spell broke, and Mum looked at me, her dark eyes wide open. My heart jolted seeing her like that – as if she'd seen a ghost. But she forced herself to smile.

'It must be a mistake. Don't worry! If the factory was closing, I'd know before the people on the radio, wouldn't I? I've been working there for eight years!' She laughed lightly and shook her head, but there was confusion in her eyes. She looked down at herself, at the work uniform she was still wearing.

Meg swallowed her sandwich. 'But they wouldn't lie on the radio!'

'Everyone makes mistakes,' Mum replied. 'Even the journalists.'

Meg sighed as if to say she doubted that very much, and she disappeared to the bedroom, her sandwich in her hand. Mum took her plate and washed it over and over in the sink, as if her mind was far, far away.

'We'll be okay, won't we Mum?' I asked quietly, frightened by her silence.

'Of course we will! Of course!' But she didn't turn to look at me, she just carried on washing that same plate.

The man on the radio was right.

There were protests, and angry letters to the local paper, and meetings in the town hall. It made no difference. Crease factory closed within a fortnight, leaving a huge empty building and angry signs on the gates: DO NOT ENTER and TRESPASSERS WILL BE PROSECUTED. Nearly seventy people lost their jobs, and my mother was one of them.

Meg

The mornings were the worst.

Before she lost her job, Mum used to leave the house at the same time as us. Something would always go wrong – Sam would forget his PE kit, or we'd remember at the last minute that there was no fruit left for break time. But after Mum lost her job, she was never in a hurry to go anywhere. She'd make breakfast for us, even though we were used to helping ourselves, and she'd make sure that everything was ready for our day at school. After a few weeks, she didn't bother getting dressed in the mornings, and she'd stand by the front door in her pyjamas, yelling 'Bye! Be good!' as she waved at us.

'Do you think she's okay?' Sam asked one day.

'No,' I answered honestly, and Sam sighed. 'Mum needs something to do. She's not the kind of woman to do nothing.'

'But ... she'll get a new job soon, won't she?'

I shook my head. Sam could be so naïve sometimes. I was only twenty minutes older than him, but he seemed to think I knew so much more than him about everything.

'There are seventy people looking for jobs in this town, Sam.'

Sam looked dejected, like a dog that had just been kicked.

'Mum will be okay,' I comforted him, feeling guilty that I'd been so negative. 'But she needs to find something to do. She's never had time for herself, ever. She just doesn't know what to do with it.'

Poor Mum. She did her best. In those first weeks, she did nothing but watch bad telly all day. But after a while, she decided to get herself a library card, and she went through books in no time at all. I'd never really seen her reading a book before then, except when she read to us. But it was as if she was on a mission to work her way through all the books she'd missed out on.

'I didn't know you liked reading,' I said one afternoon after school. Sam and I each read one chapter of whatever books we were reading every night, and now Mum would sit between us on the sofa, the three of us engrossed in our books.

'I read a lot when I was your age,' she replied. 'All

sorts of books. But then, after leaving school, there never seemed to be time. And ... well ... I think I forgot how lovely it is when you really get lost in a story.'

'And now you have time to read again!' grinned Sam. 'That's good, isn't it?'

'All I need now is for someone to pay me for sitting on my bum, reading books,' Mum answered with a sad smile.

'You could work in the library!' said Sam.

But Mum shook her head. 'The people who work there have been to university, sweetheart. Jobs like that aren't for people like me.'

And yet, as I saw her reading her way through mountains of books, I was sure that Mum was one of the cleverest people I knew. It wasn't her fault that she never got the chance to get a degree.

Late one night, I got up to fetch myself a glass of water. I'd been tossing and turning in bed, fretting about a test I had the next day. Sam was fast asleep in the top bunk.

Mum was sitting on the sofa with a blanket over her legs, her head in a book. 'Are you all right, sweetheart?'

'I just wanted some water.' I sat beside her and sipped my drink, before setting it down on the coffee table. 'Is it a good book?'

'Brilliant,' Mum smiled. 'I love this author.'

'What's it about?'

'Well, there's a woman living alone, and a tall, dark and handsome stranger turns up and whisks her off her feet.' Mum frowned. 'I'm not sure why I like it so much, actually.'

I thought about Dad. He was tall, dark and

handsome, and had startlingly blue sparking eyes. I once heard his mother, my Nan, saying, 'You'd forgive Al anything as long as those blue eyes are looking at you.' I couldn't see what eye colour had to do with anything. I wondered, would Mum still forgive him now, just because he was so handsome?

'There are more important things than looks,' I said firmly. Mum laughed and put down her book.

'You're right there. It's only a story, sweetheart.' She put her arm around me. 'What's on your mind?'

I could have told her. I could have said that I was terrified that she'd never find another job. That Sam was becoming more childish each day and that I was fed up of looking after him. That I wanted to scream at Dad for leaving us like he did, but that he wasn't here, he was never here for me to scream at him.

'Just the test tomorrow,' I said, getting up. 'Good night, Mum.'

'Good night, sweetheart.'

Sam

On that day, Meg was the first to arrive home after school. I'd walked back with Oli, and he was always slow. He wanted to show me his new bike, and I had to admire the metal and tyres and act like I was really impressed with it all. It looked exactly like his old bike to me.

When I arrived home, the sound of laughter tinkled down from Mum's room. I plucked an apple from the bowl, and went to see what all the racket was about.

Mum was standing in front of the long mirror,

holding a long grey dress in front of her. Meg was elbow-deep in the chest of drawers, occasionally pulling something out and inspecting it.

'It's all so old-fashioned!' Meg moaned, before unearthing a sparkly sand-coloured short dress. I couldn't imagine Mum wearing something like that - she lived in her jeans.

'It was very trendy once,' Mum giggled. Meg got up and held the dress up in front of Mum.

'It's so short!' Meg said reproachfully. 'When did you wear this kind of thing?'

Mum sighed. 'When I was younger. Before I had children. I never imagined, when I bought that dress, that my own daughter would look down her nose at it one day!'

'Oh, come on. It's the colour of cat sick.' Mum couldn't help but laugh, and I giggled too.

'Oh, okay. It's not the prettiest dress,' Mum admitted. 'To be honest, I was never sure about it.'

'Why do you keep it, then?' I asked, sitting on the bed.

'Well ... ' Mum became serious, her smile fading. 'That's the dress I was wearing when I met your dad.'

There was a silence, and Meg pulled the dress away from Mum. 'You should throw it away.'

Mum shook her head, and everyone was silent for a while.

'Anyway! You're meant to be helping me, Meg, but you're doing a terrible job of it.' Mum smiled again. 'I think I'll have to wear this grey suit. It's a bit tight, but I don't have anything else that's suitable for an interview ...'

I sat up straighter. 'You've got an interview?'

'Tomorrow, at the Teapot,' Meg answered on her behalf, grinning widely at Mum.

'That's great!' I exclaimed, my mouth full of apple. 'Will you get a discount?' I loved the food in the Teapot cafe in town.

'Don't get too excited. There are probably loads of people being interviewed. And I haven't waited on tables since I was a schoolgirl.'

'You mustn't think like that,' scolded Meg. 'You must have a chance, or they wouldn't have given you an interview. Now … ' She searched through a pile of clothes and found a pair of black trousers and a white shirt. 'These are perfect for an interview at the Teapot. Don't wear a suit; it's too formal.'

Mum turned to me. 'I agree with Meg,' I said.

'There we are, then,' murmured Mum, holding the clothes against her body and looking at her reflection in the mirror.

I took a long time to sleep that night. There were lots of things on my mind. I had watched the news that evening, and I could never sleep after doing that. But more than that, I couldn't help but imagine Mum working in the Teapot. It was a small cafe, and it looked a bit like a living room in an old folks' home. Swirly garish carpets, striped wall paper, and photos of lakes and deer on the walls. But the food was cheap and tasty. Dad had taken me and Meg there a few times, before he left.

I imagined Mum carrying hot plates from the kitchen and setting them down in front of hungry customers. Everyone would adore her – she was so happy and smiley. And at the end of the shift, she'd probably bring me a plate of leftovers – sausages and hash browns and fried mushrooms. The owners would surely give her a pay rise almost immediately, and they'd say, 'Karen Hughes has transformed our business completely. The cafe would be nothing without her'. And then, in a few years, I'd get a Saturday job there, where I'd learn how to cook, and I'd become a world famous chef, and ...

I slept that night with the taste of sausages in my mouth.

The next day, Meg and I ran home from school. Mum was sitting at the kitchen table, sipping a cuppa, still wearing her black trousers and white blouse. She looked up as we burst in.

'Well?' asked Meg.

'Well what?' said Mum. She had worn a little make-up for her interview, and she looked like a different version of herself.

'You got the job, didn't you?' I said happily. She looked so contented, so comfortable. But she shook her head.

'They haven't phoned yet.'

'But it went well?'

Mum nodded. 'They were nice people. It wasn't as awful as I'd thought.'

Meg grinned. 'I bet you'll get it! Oh Mum, working in the Teapot will be so much better than slaving away in that factory ... '

'Don't get so excited,' Mum said, looking worried. 'I haven't been offered the job yet. They may be looking for someone younger, or someone with more experience ... And I'm sure many people had their eye on that job.'

It was an odd evening. Meg went out with Jess, but

she came back every five minutes to check if the people from the Teapot had rung yet. I played a game on the computer, but I switched the sound off in case we wouldn't hear the phone ringing. Everyone was quiet at supper time, except when Mum said, 'I don't want you to expect too much. They might not ring at all.'

After supper, Meg and I settled by the kitchen table to do our homework. She was copying my answers, but I didn't argue like I usually do. Mum had her nose in another novel, but I could tell that her mind wasn't really on it. She picked up her phone every now and again to see if it was still working.

I had just finished my work and was packing my books into my bag when the phone rang. We all looked at one another.

'It's them,' said Mum, recognizing the number on the screen.

'Answer it, then!' yelped Meg. I felt sick. Mum pressed the green button to answer the call.

I watched her face as she listened, and I tried to guess what was being said. Mum nodded, and said 'yes, me too,' and then 'Yes, alright,' before finishing with 'Thank you for letting me know.'

There was a silence. Mum looked down. 'I didn't get the job.'

I moved to the sofa and put my arm around her. I didn't do that very often any more, I felt too old, but this was a special occasion. 'I'm sorry, Mum.'

'They're nuts!' said Meg. 'You're perfect for that job. Their business would have doubled.'

Mum smiled sadly. 'It's okay. There'll be another job, another interview.'

'A better job!' I said.

'Loads better,' Meg agreed. 'The Teapot is rubbish, anyway. The ketchup tastes like vinegar and the sausages are like sawdust.'

'And they don't keep the cans in the fridge, so the pop is always warm,' I added, though I'd loved the Teapot until that point.

'You're sweet kids,' said Mum. She looked as if she might cry. But Meg is brilliant at cheering people up, and she said,

'You would have come home stinking of fat, Mum. And your skin and hair would have been all greasy.'

Mum chuckled.

'And all the leftovers would have made you put weight on,' I said. 'And then you'd have had to spend all your wages on a new wardrobe.'

Mum grinned, and she didn't look as if she was about to cry any more.

Rent
Council Tax
Gas (central heating and hot water)
Food
Electric
Water
Telephone
Television Licence
Broadband connection
School trips
Pocket money

Meg

I think we realised how serious the situation was somewhere between the interview for the chip shop and the one for the nursing home.

Mum, Sam and I had tried to be more sensible after what happened with the Teapot. I think Mum's pride was hurt when she didn't get the job, and she became a bit quiet and withdrawn for a while. But she still spent every evening on the laptop on job sites, and bought the newspaper every Thursday, when it came with a jobs' section. In a few weeks, she got another interview. She didn't get that job, or the next. The three of us would try not to get our hopes up, but I couldn't help that little flash of excitement in my stomach when the phone rang after an interview. And I couldn't help the horrible dark feeling that came when I saw the disappointment on Mum's face yet again as she said, 'Oh, well, next time.'

One Saturday morning, with the disappointment of not getting the job in the chip shop still smarting, I found Mum sitting by the kitchen table, surrounded by envelopes and papers. She was on the phone saying, 'Not this month, but I have another job interview next week, so maybe ... '

I helped myself to some toast, and settled by the table. Mum listened to whoever was on the phone, and said, 'I just need one more month. I will have found something by then.'

It didn't sound like a very pleasant call. 'I know I couldn't pay last month either, but I lost my job unexpectedly six weeks ago ... I'll be on my feet again soon,' said Mum, her forehead creased with worry. 'OK, OK, I understand. Yes, I'll have to cancel it.' After a while, she ended the call, and sat back heavily in her chair.

'Is everything okay?' I asked lightly, though it was obvious that is wasn't at all okay.

'I can't afford the extra channels on the telly.'

'Well, they're mostly rubbish anyway.'

'But Sam likes watching the nature programmes, doesn't he?'

'Oh Mum,' I said. 'It's not a big deal.'

She sat in silence for a while before asking, 'Where is your brother?'

'Still in bed,' I replied. 'He was snoring like a train

earlier.'

'Go and wake him up, please,' she said. 'I need to speak to you both.'

I'm a level-headed person. I'm not a worrier like Sam. But I must admit that hearing Mum saying that shook me up a bit. Her voice was so flat.

By the time I'd woken Sam and dragged him to the kitchen, Mum had tidied the papers and had made a cup of tea. Sam sat beside her, wearing nothing but boxer shorts and a T-shirt, his eyes glazed as if he was still asleep.

'What's going on?' he asked, stifling a yawn.

'I want to speak to you both,' Mum answered. Sam seemed to wake up properly then, shocked by the seriousness of her voice.

'Are you ill?' he asked immediately. Poor Sam, that was the kind of thing he worried about pointlessly at night.

Mum shook her head. 'I'm perfectly healthy.'

'Are you expecting a baby?'

Mum laughed, her eyes wide with surprise. 'Expecting a baby?! What made you think ... ? Sam! You need a man to make a baby!'

'I was only asking,' my brother mumbled, blushing a bit that he'd asked such a stupid question.

'What's up then, Mum?' I asked. Mum's smile faded and she took a sip of her tea.

'Well ... it's money. Or the lack of it, actually.'

All those papers on the table must have been bills.

'I thought I'd have a new job by now, but I have to face it that maybe I won't find anything for a while. And in the meantime, money is tight. Very tight.'

'Mum's getting rid of the extra TV channels,' I told Sam.

'Oh! That doesn't matter!' he answered, relieved. Mum's seriousness had frightened him. 'It doesn't matter at all.'

'That's not all,' Mum admitted with a sigh. 'We'll have to cut back on everything – electric, gas, food. It won't be easy. But we have no choice.'

'Don't you get more money from the government because you've lost your job?' asked Sam.

'Yes, but it isn't a lot. By the time I've paid the rent, and council tax, and the water bill, and the groceries and all the rest ... well. We're spending more money than we have.'

'How do we save money, then?' I asked. I was determined to solve this problem, and make everything all right again.

Mum fetched a pen and paper. 'I'll make a list of what we spend.'

Rent
Council Tax
Gas (central heating and hot water)
Food
Electric
Water
Telephone
Television Licence
Broadband connection
School trips
Pocket money

'I've already cut the extra channels on the telly,' Mum explained. 'But what else can we save on?'

The list didn't give me much hope. We couldn't really get rid of anything on there.

'We could grow our own vegetables,' said Sam.

Mum nodded, before saying, 'That's a good idea, sweetheart, but we can't do that until next spring. But there are other ways of saving on food.'

'No takeaways,' I said flatly, thinking of how much I loved chicken tikka masala and rice.

Mum nodded. 'And we'll have to cut back on meat, it's so expensive. No ready meals. Lots of soup. Porridge for breakfast.'

'Oh please, Mum. I hate porridge.'

Mum looked at me without a trace of a smile. 'It's not my favourite food, either, but we have to sacrifice a few things for a while.'

Porridge. Yuck. When I was younger, I'd read a story about a little girl who found maggots in her porridge, and I'd never been able to enjoy it since. Every time I saw a bowlful of porridge, my eyes would search it for tiny little wriggling things.

'Your lunchboxes will have to be simpler, too.'

That's when I started feeling annoyed. So, I was going to have a horrible breakfast, followed by a boring lunch? Were we really that poor that we'd have to go hungry?

'What about the other things on the list?' Sam asked. I think that he was trying to change the subject in case Mum decided that we would only be getting bread and water for supper.

'I can't change the rent or the council tax, but there are ways to save on gas and electricity. When the cold weather comes, we'll put on a few jumpers instead of putting the heating on. We'll have showers only every other day. And it's easy to cut back on electricity – I'll hang the washing on the line instead of using the drier, and I won't wash clothes as often. We're not to use the dishwasher, we'll wash up in the sink. No leaving the telly or radio on when we're not paying attention to them – I'm always doing that.'

'Anything else?' I asked sarcastically. It sounded like hard work to me. I could imagine myself, starving while washing the dishes, my hair and clothes caked with dirt.

'Yes.' Mum stared straight at me, sensing my disapproval. 'If you leave a room, you have to turn out the light. Light uses a lot of electricity.'

I imagined myself, starving while washing the dishes, my hair and clothes caked in dirt. *In the dark*.

Sam

I knew Meg was annoyed. She isn't very good at hiding her feelings, and she'd ben stomping around the house and slamming doors. She can sulk for days. Weeks, sometimes. But she always loses her temper in the end, and I knew there was a storm coming.

I'd seen her face when she opened her lunch box at school a few days earlier. She looked as if someone had stolen her food and put dirt in its place. And all right, our lunches weren't as tasty as they used to be, but at least they filled us up.

Our lunch boxes used to be like this:

A ham sandwich
Some cheese in red wax
A bag of small crackers, salt-and-vinegar-flavoured
Grapes
Yogurt

It was the same kind of food most kids in our class got, except for the lucky few who were fortunate enough to get crisps and sweets and chocolate, and Nell Davies who was allergic to practically everything and had salad with lemon juice every single day.

After Mum made the changes, this is what we had:

A cheese sandwich
Carrot batons
Nuts or raisins (Mum bought them in huge packets and we had a small amount in little plastic boxes.)
Homemade flapjack.

It didn't look very appetising, but it tasted okay.

Meg didn't think so. 'I'm embarrassed to open my lunch box in front of my friends!' she said one day as we walked home from school. 'It's not fair!'

'Don't say that to Mum. It's not her fault.'

'I know that. But it's not our fault, either. Why do idiots like Jon get two sandwiches, a bag of crisps, cake and pop, and we get this? And he doesn't even eat half of what he's given!'

It was true. Just the day before, I'd seen Jon

scoffing half a bar of chocolate before chucking it in the bin. I'd almost gone scavenging in the rubbish for it.

Anyway, Meg was furious about this for days, getting angrier and angrier. But her temper finally exploded at the very worst time – when Oli came over. We were in the bedroom playing a car-racing game when the sound of yelling suddenly blasted from the kitchen. I knew Meg was down there doing her homework, and Mum was making supper.

'Are they okay?' Oli asked, looking a bit anxious.

'Meg's complaining.'

'About ... ?'

'We have to spend less money now that Mum's out of a job. Meg doesn't like the fact that our lunch boxes have changed a bit.'

We played in silence for a while, listening to Meg shouting. I hadn't told him that we were poor now, because I didn't know what he'd say. His dad was a postman, and his mum worked in the Co-op. They weren't rich, like Jon's parents, but they got by.

'Your mum will get another job, you know.'

He was trying to make me feel better, but for some reason, his kindness made me feel sad.

'She's had loads of interviews. But she never gets the job.'

'But she will, one day. Your mum's really nice.'

I was glad when he said that.

'You don't understand!' yelled Meg's furious voice from downstairs, and I got up.

'Do you mind staying here for a minute, Oli? I'm going to sort her out.' He nodded, looking as though he really felt for me.

'Will you please shut up?!' I hissed in the kitchen. 'Oli is here, and you're embarrassing me!'

Meg was standing behind her chair beside the table, and Mum was standing by the stove, glowering. Actually, I thought, they'd never looked so alike.

'Oli might as well know that we're poor now! Everybody else knows! They only have to look at our lunch boxes!' Meg's eyes were fixed on Mum.

'I am doing my best … ' started Mum.

'Just leave it, Meg,' I said, seeing Mum starting to lose her temper.

Meg turned to me. 'Has Mum told you about the internet?'

'What about it?'

'We can't afford it any more! How are we supposed to do our homework without the internet?'

Mum shut her eyes, as if she was doing her very best not to lose her temper. 'It's eighteen pounds a month. We just don't have the money.'

I was quiet for a bit. If anything, I used the internet more often than Meg did. I read about different animals and read comics online and went on news websites. Meg didn't have the patience, and gave up if she couldn't find what she was looking for straight away. Losing the connection to the internet wouldn't make much of a difference to her.

'Are you sure, Mum?' I asked in a small voice. I knew things weren't easy for her, but I'd really miss the online wildlife videos, the ones with whales and crocodiles and polar bears.

Mum shook her head. 'I have no choice.'

'But what about all the websites that advertise

jobs? You're on those almost every evening … '

'I'll go to the library every day. You can use the internet for free there.' She suddenly looked very tired.

'Well, that's just great,' said Meg sarcastically. 'I'll have to walk all the way down to the library to do my homework. And it shuts at five!' She stomped upstairs and slammed her bedroom door.

Mum slumped heavily in a chair. I didn't know what to say, but I had to say something.

'It's okay, Mum. It doesn't take five minutes to walk to the library.'

Mum smiled weakly. 'I know, sweetheart.'

I didn't enjoy the rest of that Saturday. I was uneasy, even after Meg went out with Jess and Mum settled with a book. Perhaps I should have accepted Oli's offer of tea at his house, but I felt … I felt really awful.

Bored and restless, I reached for a small notebook I'd had for ages and started working out how much money we were saving on a few things. I wasn't sure of the price of everything, but Mum kept all our receipts in the bottom drawer in the kitchen, so I used those.

The lunch boxes, I decided. I'd work out the difference between the price of the lunch we had before and the ones we had now. It wasn't easy, I had to work out how long a packet of cheese would last us and that kind of thing. But I did it in the end, though I could never be sure if I was exactly right.

Ham sandwich	4 4 p
Cheese in red wax	3 8 p
Bag of crisps (salt and vinegar)	2 6 p
Grapes	4 8 p
Yogurt	8 0 p
	2 3 6 p = £2.36

Cheese sandwich	2 1 p
Carrot batons	8 p
Nuts or sultanas	1 8 p
Homemade flapjack	2 6 p
	= 7 3 p

Goodness! That saved £1.63 a day! £3.26 a day between Meg and me. And every school week was ten lunches, between us, which meant a weekly saving of £16.30!

'Hey, Mum!' I rushed into the kitchen, where she was making a cup of coffee. I waved the notebook at her. '£16.30, Mum!'

She looked at me as if I'd lost it completely. 'What?'

'I've done the sums, and we save £16.30 a week with the new lunches!'

Mum sat down, and took the notebook from my hands. She gazed open-mouthed at the sums. 'You did these?'

I nodded. 'Yes. They're not completely perfect. They're probably a few pence out. It was difficult to work out how much your flapjacks cost to make. But it's not far off! That's a huge saving, isn't it?'

Mum nodded. 'It's incredible that you've done this, Sam.'

'I was thinking maybe we could keep the internet ... ? Because we're saving so much on food ... '

Mum stared at the paper as if she didn't see it at all. She swallowed hard several times, and then when she spoke, her voice was odd.

'We have to save every penny we can, sweetheart. Change the lunches **and** get rid of the internet. I'm sorry.'

'It doesn't matter,' I answered quickly. 'It's still nice to see it written down like that, isn't it? Seeing all the money we're saving!' And I hurried from the kitchen, pretending that I hadn't realised that she was crying.

Meg

One Sunday morning, Mum decided that we were all going to have a day out together.

I think she'd become fed up of being stuck in the house all the time, doing nothing. Our argument about the internet had cooled, and things weren't as awful as I'd imagined. To be honest, I felt bad for making such a fuss about it. It couldn't be helped.

'Get up!' Mum said, throwing open the curtains. 'We're going out.'

I groaned, and pulled my pillow over my face to block out the light. 'Nooooooo … '

'Breakfast in five minutes,' Mum said firmly. 'I'm expecting you to be up, dressed and washed.'

'Just another half hour in bed,' Sam pleaded from the bottom bunk. He'd been reading in bed until the small hours.

'No! It's a beautiful day. Come on!'

Of course, neither one of us got up straight away, but Mum was determined, and she pulled the duvets from our beds and left them heaped in a corner of the bedroom. The bed wasn't very cosy without the duvet, so I got up.

After getting dressed and washing my face, I went into the kitchen and slumped into a chair. Mum was preparing a huge pile of sandwiches.

'Sandwiches for breakfast?' I asked doubtfully.

'For lunch,' she replied, wrapping them all in clingfilm and chucking them into her backpack. She threw in a few bags of crisps, too, and some bottled water.

'Where are we going?'

'Look through the window, Meg,' she said. 'What can you see?'

'Bungalows,' I answered flatly. 'Parked cars. Weeds in the garden.'

'Blue sky!' Mum was full of enthusiasm, and I couldn't help but smile. I hadn't seen her like this in a long time.

'I want to go back to bed.' Sam flopped into the chair beside mine. He was wearing his jumper inside out. 'Everyone has a lie in on a Sunday morning … '

'Poor everyone, missing out on such a beautiful day,' replied Mum as she placed two bowls of steaming porridge in front of us. 'Come on, eat up. You'll need the energy.'

By half past nine, we'd left the house and Mum was carrying the backpack. It was quiet, everyone else still in bed. We walked out of Tywyn on one of the small lanes, and in about half an hour, the church bells stared to ring. We turned and looked back at our town.

'It's pretty, isn't it?' said Sam.

And yes, it was pretty. Beautiful, actually. I'd forgotten how lucky we were to live here with hills on one side of town, and the sea on the other.

We had a lovely day. I couldn't remember the last time we'd laughed so much together ... it must have been before Mum lost her job. We walked for miles over the mountains, following paths I'd never known were there.

'You've never walked this far before,' Mum said as we reached the top of a hill.

'Even when we climbed Snowdon?' asked Sam. His cheeks were flushed from exercise and it suited him.

'We only walked up. You two and I caught the train on the way back. Don't you remember?

'I remember. Dad walked down, and the three of us went to a cafe in Llanberis and had ice cream while we waited for him.' The memory made me smile. I could only remember little details – pink ice cream; mud stains on Mum's jeans; Dad grinning when he saw us.

On one of the hills, there was an old stone circle, and that's where we sat to eat our lunch. It wasn't a feast, but I didn't think I'd ever tasted anything so wonderful.

'Thanks, Mum,' I said, my mouth full of peanut butter sandwich.

Mum looked up at me, right into my eyes. She was

leaning back on a standing stone, and she looked pretty. I had never considered her a beautiful woman – she was small and round, and she rarely dressed up or wore make-up. She always looked so plain beside Dad. But there, sitting in a stone circle in the hills, she looked perfect to me.

'You're welcome,' Mum smiled, and that's when I knew for certain that I'd been forgiven for creating that stupid argument a few weeks before.

We didn't get home until four o'clock. 'Six and a half hours of walking,' I said, pulling off my trainers and chucking them to the corner of the porch. 'My legs feel like jelly.'

'Mine, too,' Mum agreed, switching on the kettle. 'Tea! I need tea.'

Sam couldn't say a word. He collapsed, exhausted, on the sofa. Mum put the radio on, and, without even asking us, made some hot chocolate for Sam and me. It was delicious.

'I could sleep right now,' Sam said, kicking off his trainers.

'Did you have a nice day?' asked Mum, rubbing her feet.

'It was great.'

'Yes,' I agreed. I would probably have sat in the house all day doing nothing if Mum hadn't forced me to go out. And although I was tired, it was a lovely tiredness, as if I had worked hard to deserve the sleep I'd be getting later.

'I'll put a pizza in the oven. Why don't we all watch a DVD together? We'll turn out the light and draw the curtains.'

'Great!' said Sam, who loved doing homely things. But I wasn't sure. I'd planned on going over to Jess's house for a chat and a gossip. But when I saw Sam and Mum's faces staring at me expectantly, I caved in.

'Okay. But only if I get to pick the DVD.'

Sam

It was almost as good as the old days.

Up in the hills, I turned and looked at the view.
The sea was shining, and the mountains on the horizon
were dark and craggy. The flat fields around our town
looked ridiculously green, as if they'd been painted by a
child. And then there was my town, and the church in the
centre, proudly waving its Welsh dragon.

'I can see the school,' I pointed.

'And the leisure centre,' added Meg. 'And the

playing fields, and Jess's house.'

'And the old factory,' said Mum quietly, but she didn't sound sad. The factory looked peculiar – a huge square building on the edge of town, no lorries or cars in the car park.

But it was impossible to be sad as we walked in such a lovely place. The argument between Mum and Meg had been forgotten and, for a while, they walked in front of me, arm in arm, on the path. They were so different – Meg was already taller than Mum, and thin as a rake whereas Mum was wider. You'd never say they were related.

We laughed all day. Mum told us about the time she was our age, and she and her mate, Beryl, had walked from Aberdyfi to Tywyn and laughed so much at some silly joke that they wet their pants!

' ... and Beryl walked home like this ... ' Mum walked with her legs apart, looking uncomfortable as if she was cold and wet. Well, Meg and I laughed hysterically. Meg was doubled over, and when Mum said 'You watch that *you* don't pee your pants, now!,' she laughed even harder.

As we ate our picnic, I couldn't help but do the sums in my head.

Peanut butter sandwich	38p
Crisps	20p
Apple	30p
	= 88p

Our lovely day out had only cost about 88p each.

And we'd still have had lunch, even if we'd been at home, and we probably would have used electricity, too. So, in a way, our day had been free. A part of me wanted to say that to Mum and Meg, but I wasn't sure whether that was the right thing to do. Maybe they didn't want to be reminded of how poor we were.

Later on, as we sat on the sofa watching a film we'd all seen loads of times before, I had a feeling that I don't get very often.

I felt that everything was going to be all right.

Meg

'No way, never ever, I won't, I will not,' I said firmly. I was getting ready for school, rushing around, trying to find things. 'Have you seen my reading book?'

'It's on top of the microwave,' replied Mum, and I grabbed the book and stuffed it into my bag. 'You have to go, Meg. She wants to see you both.'

'No, she doesn't,' Sam grumbled, putting on his coat. 'She just feels guilty because she hasn't bothered with us for so long.'

'Exactly!' It was good having Sam agreeing with me, for once. He rarely complained about anything, but he could moan about Nan for hours.

'It's difficult for her to see you as much as she wants to. Bangor is nearly two hours away, and she doesn't like driving that far.'

'Well, she doesn't have to,' Sam offered. 'She can stay at home. It's fine by me.'

'You're going,' Mum said firmly. 'Your Nan loves you, and she's asked to spend time with you. And she's going to be staying in Aberystwyth for a few days. She'll pick you up on the way.'

'We don't have to stay with her overnight!' I exclaimed, horrified.

'No, you'll get the bus home at the end of the day. But she has a right to see you two - she is your grandmother, after all. No more arguments. This is going to happen, and it will happen on Saturday. She's picking you up at nine.'

'In the morning?!' I moaned.

'Of course, in the morning!' Mum shook her head. 'School, now. Or you'll be late.'

Nan was my father's mother, and she lived in a posh old house on the outskirts of Bangor. Her husband, my grandfather, had died years ago, and Dad was their only child.

When Dad still lived with us, Nan would sometimes come to stay. She was an elegant lady, always dressed in bright colours and lots of jewellery, and I'd never seen her without make-up. When I was a little girl, I used to think she was okay. She didn't play with us, like other people's grandparents, or take us to Burger Land or to the sweet shop, but I didn't mind too much. But as I got older, I started to notice the way she looked at our house, as though it wasn't good enough, and the way she raised an eyebrow at Mum's cooking as if there was anything the matter with curry and rice.

The last time she came to stay, not long before Dad legged it, I decided that I really didn't like her at all. There were a few reasons, but the main one was when I heard her saying to Mum, 'Don't you think Meg is exactly like my side of the family, Karen? Tall and willowy. And those dark eyes! And poor Sam, he takes after your side. Doesn't he like exercise at all?' The mean old crow.

After Dad left, we never saw her. It was one of the positive things about him leaving us. But she phoned every now and then, sounding terribly snobbish as usual. And now, we had to spend an entire day in her company.

'Yoo-hoo!' Nan's voice filled the house, and I ground my teeth. She was already getting on my nerves. I promised myself that I would never ever yell 'yoo-hoo' as I arrived at anyone's house, not for as long as I lived.

She was standing in the kitchen, having let herself in. 'Meg!' she cried, wrapping me in her arms. I nearly choked at the overpowering stink of her perfume. 'Goodness, how you've grown! You're exactly like I was when I was your age.' God help me.

Sam came in wearing a smile, fair play to him. Nan didn't give him a hug like she'd given me. 'Sammy! How are you, darling?' Nobody called him Sammy. Sammy was a dog's name.

Then Mum came in, and there were a few seconds of

awkward silence. 'How are you?' Mum asked quietly, and I hated Nan for making Mum feel so shy. 'Wonderful, diolch, Karen. And you?'

'Fine, thanks.'

'Never mind about the job, eh? People always need workers like you.'

That sounded like a mean thing to say, though I couldn't work out why.

'Are you ready to go?' asked Nan. The sapphires on her dangly earrings shone as she moved her head, and her coat twinkled with glitter and sequins. She looked like Christmas.

'Okay,' said Sam. His voice was completely flat.

'All right,' I added.

'Wonderful! Your mother will have all day to clean the house.'

It takes an hour to get to Aberystwyth from our house in Tywyn. By the time we'd reached Machynlleth, I wanted to scream at Nan.

She was trying to convince Sam to take up rugby. He wasn't at all interested in sports. P.E. was the only lesson in school that he truly hated.

'Al was in both the rugby and football teams at school,' said Nan. Her voice always became soft when she was talking about Dad.

'Sam prefers to read and do his homework. He's the smartest boy in our class,' I said from the back seat. Sam would never brag, so I had to do it for him.

'Al was wonderful at his lessons, too,' Nan answered, smiling at me in the rearview mirror. 'His reports were a joy to behold.' She looked sideways at Sam in the passenger seat. 'So it *is* possible to be good at everything, you see?'

'I like walking,' said Sam in a small voice.

Nan laughed as if that was a joke. 'Going for a stroll isn't a sport!'

'Yes, it is,' I said, and ignored the fact that Nan was looking at me in the mirror again.

Prawn salad	£ 4.90
Posh chicken and chips	£11.80
Chocolate pudding	£ 4.95
	= £21.65

Sam

She was even worse than usual.

It felt as if she was on a mission to spend as much as she could. She went to the pay and display car park, though I told her where she could park for free. 'But it's further from the town centre! I don't want to walk more than necessary in these heels, darling.' £4.60 just for parking! We were nearly a fiver down before even reaching the shops!

'Now,' she said, as she led us to an expensive-looking clothes shop. 'Get whatever you want. Don't think about the expense.'

Meg nodded, looking quite jolly. I managed to sneak a private word with her while Nan's attention was diverted to the sparkly jewellery at the other end of the shop.

'Are you going to let her buy you these clothes?!' I asked. 'She's terrible!'

'Exactly,' replied Meg, taking a hoodie off the rail. 'She *is* terrible, and so I won't feel guilty for accepting her presents.'

'There's something sly about that,' I said, unsure.

Meg turned her dark eyes on me. 'Listen, Sam. You've just sat in that car for a whole hour, listening to her being openly rude to you. You deserve a whole new wardrobe just for not screaming at her to shut up.'

I sighed.

'Okay, think of it like this,' Meg went on. 'You need new clothes. If Nan doesn't buy them, Mum will have to.' Meg reached for a pair of jogging trousers. 'You're saving Mum money by letting Nan buy stuff for you.'

She was right. I smiled at her, and started searching the rails for something that took my fancy. Nan returned to us.

'Oh dear me, no, Meg. We want pretty clothes – dresses, skirts, something with a bit of glitz. Put those sporty clothes back, darling. And Sam, why don't we look for something that will flatter your physique ... something black, perhaps ... ?'

Meg and I fancied a burger for lunch. I couldn't remember the last time we'd had fast food. It was months since Mum had lost her job, and we'd lived on cheap food since then and hadn't had a single takeaway. I felt hopeful when Nan said, 'Right then! How about a spot of lunch? You can choose where – anywhere at all!'

'Burger Land,' replied Meg.

'Or a pizza place!'

'Oh dear. Obviously, I'll have to choose. I know where we'll go.'

The restaurant was called Deliciosa, and I'd never been anywhere like it. The waiter wore a black suit with a bow tie, as if he was about to sing in an opera instead of just fetching pop for Meg and me and a glass of wine for Nan.

'And remember to have a starter, and dessert too,' Nan smiled at us over the menu. I couldn't believe the prices. One goat's cheese and red onion tart, which was only a starter, cost more than a burger, chips and drink from a fastfood restaurant.

The food was nice. I can't pretend that it was good value, though. As I looked down at my *chicken goujons with twice-baked Anglesey potato chips*, which was basically posh chicken nuggets and chips, I kept thinking, 'Is this really worth £11.80?' It was nice, but not that nice.

Throughout the meal, Nan went on and on about Dad. Reminiscing about when he was a schoolboy, and how kind and clever and handsome he was. I saw Meg having to actually press her lips tightly together so that she didn't make some sarcastic remark.

'Has he told you about this new job in Cardiff? Goodness, he's done well. Area manager, and he travels around everywhere, telling people what to do. He hasn't mentioned it, but I'm sure he's making a great deal of money.' Of course, Meg and I had no idea about any of this

- Dad hadn't been in touch for months. I didn't know that he was living in Cardiff. It was odd to think of him in a big city, living in a place I'd never seen.

As we were scoffing the chocolate pudding (which was, I admit, almost worth the £4.95 they were charging for it) Nan said, 'Right then, darlings! What else do you need?'

'You've already bought us loads,' I replied, looking at all the bags on the floor beside me.

'But I want to spoil you! That's what grandmothers are for!' She looked at our feet. 'Shoes?'

By the time Nan said goodbye to us by the bus, Meg and I had as much as we could carry. Huge plastic bags full of clothes, shoes, jewellery for Meg and books for me. Nan had spent a fortune.

'Goodbye. Thank you for spending the day with me. I hope you enjoyed yourselves.'

'Thanks for all the stuff,' I replied, feeling that saying thanks wasn't really enough.

Nan kissed me briefly on the cheek. 'I'll see you soon.'

'Thank you, Nan,' Meg reached over and kissed her. I was about to disappear into the bus when Meg added, 'Say hello to Dad, if you speak to him.'

'What?' asked Nan, as if she couldn't understand.

'If you speak to Dad,' Meg repeated.

'But doesn't he ring you..?' Nan asked.

'We'd better go,' said Meg as the bus engine started to whine. 'But tell him I'm glad to hear of his new job.'

She was grinning widely by the time she collapsed into the seat in front of mine on the bus. 'You knew exactly what you were doing, saying that to her,' I said reproachfully, but I couldn't help myself from smiling.

'I couldn't stand listening to her going on about how perfect Dad is. Maybe she'll realise now that he isn't such a golden boy.'

In the bus on the way home, I reached into my pocket for a pencil, and wrote a sum on the back of one of the receipts. I worked out exactly how much Nan had paid for my lunch.

Prawn salad	£ 4 . 90
Posh chicken and chips	£ 11 . 80
Chocolate pudding	£ 4 . 95
	= £ 2 1 . 6 5

Over twenty quid! That would pay for my lunch box for a whole month!

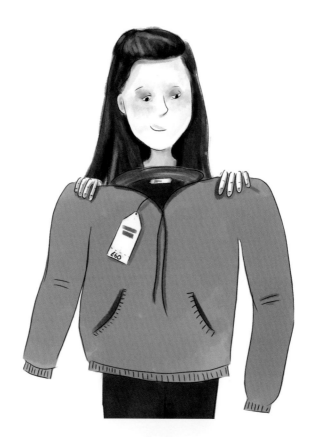

Meg

Mum's mouth dropped open when she saw us stepping off
the bus with all our bags. 'Wow,' she said weakly, giving
me and Sam a kiss each. 'Was there anything left in the
shops, or did you buy it all?'

She took a few of our bags and we walked home.
I must admit that I was exhausted. And I might as well be
honest, I did feel the tiniest bit guilty about saying those
things to Nan as I got on the bus. It wasn't her fault that
she thought that Dad was perfect – he was her son, after

all.

'What did you do while we were gone?' I asked Mum, trying to take my mind off it.

'I cleaned the house.'

'You didn't listen to Nan!' Sam exclaimed. 'The house didn't need cleaning! And anyway, what would she know? Nan has a cleaning lady! She doesn't have to clean anything herself!'

'Hey, now,' Mum said, with a warning tone in her voice. 'I don't want to hear you speaking ill of your grandmother. Especially when she's just spent an absolute fortune on you. She adores you both. Now, hurry up so that we can get home – I want to see what you've got! It's like Christmas!'

After making a cup of tea for Mum and squash for Sam and myself, the three of us sat in the living room, emptying the shopping bags. Mum stroked the soft material and raised it to her nose so that she could smell that lovely, brand new scent. Then the price tag caught her eye.

'£60! £60 for a hoodie!' She stared at the price tag as if there was a mistake.

'I know.' I rolled my eyes. 'Nan refused to even look in the cheaper shops. She didn't really want to buy that hoodie, either! She said it made me look like a boy.' I frowned at the memory.

Sam chuckled as he reached into one of his bags. 'Nan was trying to convince Meg that what she really wanted was a long pink dress, covered in glittery butterflies.' I made a sick noise. I would never, ever wear anything like that.

'£55 for jeans?' Mum exclaimed. 'And they're full

of holes!'

'They're meant to be like that,' said Sam. 'And look at these trainers, Mum! They're exactly the same ones as Jon has.' He disappeared into the bedroom to change.

For a moment, I thought that Mum was going to faint. She'd just seen the receipt. 'Don't worry, Mum. That's just how much trainers cost these days.'

'But he grows so quickly! These trainers will only fit him for a few months!'

Sam came back, grinning proudly. He was wearing his new jeans, new trainers, new T-shirt and hoodie, and a new cap. He didn't look like Sam at all. 'You look great,' said Mum, and she looked like she meant it, too.

She didn't mention the price of our new things again. She only said how great we looked in our new clothes, and admired my new jewellery and flicked through Sam's new books. When Sam said that Nan had left the receipts in the bags so that we could exchange them for something else if we wanted, Mum swept them up without looking at them, and folded them into her back pocket.

We only wanted beans on toast for supper – we were still full after the feast in the restaurant. I couldn't be bothered to do much that evening - I was so tired – so I did my homework early for once, and watched rubbish on telly. We all went to bed early. Sam lay in the bottom bed, scribbling into his notebook as I read a book.

'Sam?'

The sound of scribbling stopped. 'Yes?'

'Do you think Mum was a bit quiet tonight?'

'Yes.' We both thought about it. I didn't usually

worry like this - Sam was the one who did that.

'Do you think she's upset that Nan bought us all that stuff?'

'No. But I think I know what's wrong with her.' He sighed. 'She feels bad that she can't afford to buy us things like that.'

'But I don't care about that! Well, not most of the time, anyway.'

'Look.' Sam passed his notebook up to me. He'd neatly written a sum on the lined paper. 'It's not exactly right – it may be a few pounds out. And I had to guess how much your meal cost.'

Clothes for Meg:	
Hoodie	£ 60
Trousers	£ 50
Jumper	£ 50
Skirt	£ 45
Trainers	£ 97
Clothes for Sam:	
Hoodie	£ 60
Jeans	£ 55
T-shirt	£ 35
Cap	£ 20
Trainers	£ 103
Books for Sam	£ 36.94
Jewellery for Meg	£ 32.56
Lunch for Sam	£ 21.65
Lunch for Meg	£ 21.65
Total	= £687.80

'No way!' I sat up in bed. 'Nearly seven hundred pounds! There must be a mistake ... '

'I've done the sum three times,' replied Sam. 'That's how much Nan spent on us today.'

The whole thing made me feel ill. I knew she'd spent a lot, but this was a fortune.

I thought of her face as the bus pulled away. I regretted letting her know that Dad never phoned us. Though she could be a mean old crow, she must have loved us to have spent so much.

'Do you think we should take the things back and exchange them for money? Then we could give it to Mum.' I didn't want to – I loved the new things – but spending £687.80 on clothes and jewellery felt ridiculous when we were so poor.

'Mum would never let us do that,' said Sam. 'But she had the receipts, so she knows how much was spent. And Mum buys all her clothes from the charity shop in town. I don't think she's spent more than £50 on an item of clothing since she bought her wedding dress.'

'Poor Mum.' I lay back in bed, and Sam turned out the light.

'The thing is, Meg, our monthly rent for this house is £450, and Nan can afford to spend nearly £700 in a single day. I bet Mum feels terrible.'

Sam

In no time at all, autumn had arrived. Nothing changed in our house – Mum still hadn't found a job, Dad still hadn't phoned, and the half term holidays went by without us doing much. I'd been nervous that Nan might get in touch to try and get Meg and me to go and stay with her to Bangor for a few days, but she didn't, thank goodness.

And then it became very cold.

It was November by then, and we'd been coping with the drop in temperature by wearing thick jumpers and several pairs of socks, as well as piling our beds with two or three duvets each. But in November, it became colder still, and simply wearing more clothes didn't work any more.

In the beginning, we all pretended not to notice. Meg and I knew how expensive it was to switch on the central heating – Mum had told us months ago – and even last year, when Mum was working, she was still loath to switch on the heating. So for a few weeks, we suffered in silence. No one wanted to be the one who suggested it was time to push the little red button that fired up the boiler.

Honestly, it was horrible. I'd been cold before, of course, while going for walks in winter or throwing snowballs, or that time I forgot to take my coat to school and the temperature dropped by the time we went home. But being cold in the house felt completely different. It didn't feel so much like home, somehow.

In the morning, I'd wake up to see my breath rising from my mouth, and it has to be very cold for that to happen. Then, I'd get up and change into my school uniform as quickly as I could. More often than not, my clothes felt damp because they'd been cold for so long, and they were horribly uncomfortable.

'My clothes feel as if they've just come straight out of the washing machine!' moaned Meg one morning after pulling on her shirt. I was nervous, then, that she'd say something to Mum about putting the central heating on, so I tried to think of a solution as quickly as I could.

'If we keep our clothes under the bedsheets with us, they'll be lovely and warm by morning.'

Meg looked at me as if I'd lost it, and she mumbled something under her breath. But that evening, she folded her uniform and parcelled it in the foot of her bed, and I did the same. The next morning, we both changed into our clothes while we were still in bed, and everything was warm and dry. Though Meg never said anything, I felt quite proud of myself.

But I couldn't solve every problem. I hated the feeling of seeing Mum sitting on the sofa, reading, wearing a coat, hat and gloves. I didn't like seeing frost on the inside of the windows in the mornings. I couldn't make a real difference. I hated coming home from school and keeping my coat on all evening. Meg started to spend most of her evenings at Jess' house. When the library was open, Mum would go there and sit by the radiator, reading. I'd go to bed early every night, doing my homework under the duvet – it was warmer that way.

At the beginning of December, I thought Meg was going to crack. She'd stay out as long as possible, and barely looked at Mum or me, as if it was our fault that gas was so expensive. One Sunday morning, as she was doing her homework by the kitchen table, she threw down her biro and exclaimed, 'I can't do this any more! My hand is shivering so much that I can't write! This is ridiculous. There must be a way of making enough money to put the heating on. We'll all get ill if we go on like this ...'

And it was at that exact moment that the phone rang.

Meg

'It's your father,' said Mum, staring in surprise at the name that flashed up on her phone.

'Dad?' repeated Sam, as if Dad was someone important and powerful like a film star or a singer in a band.

Mum nodded silently, and passed the phone to Sam.

'I don't want to speak to him,' I said, just as Sam was pressing the button to answer the call. I turned on my heel as Sam's meek voice bleated a pathetic 'Hello?' I didn't want to hear their conversation.

Mum followed me to the bedroom, and sat in the little chair by the bookshelf. I jumped up to the top bunk bed and pretended to read. She said nothing. I couldn't stand the tension for long. 'If there's something you want to say, Mum, just say it.'

Mum shook her head. 'Nothing.'

'Why are you in my bedroom, then?'

'I wanted Sam to be able to speak to his dad in private.'

'You could have gone to your own bedroom.' I turned my back on her. 'I won't speak to him.'

There was a short pause, and then Mum said, 'You don't have to. Nobody's going to force you.'

'Well ... thank goodness for that.' I was surprised. I'd been sure that Mum was going to try and persuade me.

Sam was on the phone for about five minutes before coming in to the bedroom. 'I'll ask her now,' he said into the phone, then turned to me. 'Dad wants to speak to you.'

'No thanks,' I replied, my throat starting to feel tight. Sam stood for a while, staring at me.

'But he's asking ... '

'I don't want to speak to him, Sam.' My voice didn't sound like mine.

'Meg is busy at the moment, Dad,' said Sam, and then, 'No, no, she's okay. She's just ... ' He wasn't brave enough to finish the sentence.

'I'm not busy,' I growled at Sam. 'I just don't want to speak to him.'

'Dad's asking to speak to you,' said Sam to Mum, and she nodded, looking tired. 'Okay, Dad. Bye, then. All right, Dad. Bye.'

Mum took the phone into the kitchen to speak to Dad, and Sam sat in her chair. His movements looked somehow heavy, his face pale.

'What did he say?' I ventured, and hated myself for asking.

'Nothing much. Asked how we were, how's school, that kind of thing.'

I shook my head angrily. 'It's none of his business.'

'He asked about Oli, and about you, and he said he thinks about us all the time. He's got a new flat in Cardiff. He has a photo of us on the mantelpiece.'

'It's an old photo, Sam. He doesn't have any recent ones. He hasn't seen us to take any photos.'

'But he hasn't forgotten about us, either.' Sam turned his eyes to mine. He usually looked so young. People always thought he was years younger than me. But then, after speaking to Dad on the phone, his eyes seemed old, as if he'd seen too many things.

'What's the point in remembering us if he doesn't see us? He's not behaving like a father should … ' But it was as if Sam couldn't hear me at all.

'Do you know what the strangest thing was, Meg? He sounded like he always did. As if he was just phoning on the way back from work to ask if we needed something from the shop. I'd almost forgotten what he sounds like.'

As soon as Sam said that, a silly memory sprung into my mind - Dad returning home from work every day, and loosening his tie as he sat by the kitchen table. He'd say to me, *Hey Meg, Daddy's girl, light of my life* … And if I was in a good mood I'd laugh, but if I was miserable I'd just pout. Dad would always laugh, never mind how

I reacted. That was the kind of man he was. Always laughing.

I didn't sleep much that night. My mind kept going back to Dad, plus I was freezing. I kept remembering stupid pointless little things – the way Dad liked his toast almost burnt, like me; the way he sang in the shower; the way he drove away from our home, without once looking back.

Sam

It was Mum who said it, in the end. I hadn't expected that, but it was a relief.

'I know the house is cold. I feel it, too. It's become an unwelcoming place, and I don't want that.'

We were gulping our breakfast so that we could get to school in time. Looking around the table, Mum was obviously right. We all wore hats and coats, and Mum was wearing a pair of woolly mittens. It was December, after all.

'It's too cold to have a shower,' said Meg. 'Thank goodness that the school takes us swimming, or I'd stink.'

'I know, sweetheart,' said Mum. 'But heating the house is expensive. I have some money put to one side, but … '

'Oh please!' pleaded Meg. 'I'd do anything!'

'The thing is,' said Mum, 'it's the money I've put by for your birthday trip.'

Meg shut up then. She looked at me, and then at Mum. 'Oh.'

'It's enough money to put the heating on for an hour or two in the evening, and for half an hour in the morning. Only for about three months. I've been saving everything I can for your birthday trip, you see.'

'That doesn't matter,' I said. I wasn't sure whether I believed myself. I'd been looking forward to Oak Park – had been thinking of it as the one good thing that was planned for the three of us, a time when we'd be able to forget everything.

'Use the money to heat the house,' said Meg, but her small voice told me that the trip had meant a lot to her, too. 'It's more important.'

That morning, after leaving for school, I caught a sad glimpse through the kitchen window. Mum was still sitting by the table, her head in her hands, as if the weight of the world was on her shoulders.

'It's only a birthday,' said Meg as we walked home that afternoon. 'It's not important.'

'You're right,' I agreed. 'It isn't as if we're little kids anymore. Not everyone makes a big fuss on their birthdays.'

But we were both disappointed. There are some things you can't admit to, even to your twin, and I couldn't admit to Meg how much I'd been looking forward to Oak Park.

Things weren't all bad, though. Walking into our house that afternoon was an experience I'll never forget. It was like a different place – warm and inviting. Mum had made us some hot chocolate, and she was grinning, having at last been able to remove her coat.

'Ooooh Mum!' exclaimed Meg, rushing to warm her hands on one of the radiators. 'This is wonderful!'

Mum smiled. 'It is, isn't it? I can't remember the last time I took off my coat!'

After we finished the hot chocolate, and after Meg and I had fetched our homework books to the kitchen table, I realised something. 'I didn't feel this happy when we put the heating on last year.'

'Well, maybe you have to go without something for a while in order to really appreciate it,' said Meg.

And at that second, that precise second in my life, I wouldn't have changed a single thing. I was perfectly happy.

Meg

<u>Christmas List</u>
Laptop
Phone
New dress

I never showed Mum my real Christmas list. One afternoon, on the computer in the library, I went online to see how much things cost. You couldn't buy a laptop for less than £300, and any phone worth having cost at least half that.

Only the dress stayed on my list, and I added a few other things – a hot water bottle, biros, lip gloss. Things you could get from the pound shop.

Jess was with me in the library. I hadn't told her what things were like in our house – I think I was embarrassed. But she'd noticed little things, like how cold the house was before Mum finally put the heating on, and how pathetic my lunch box looked now. Her family didn't have much money, either – her parents couldn't find work, and she had three little brothers. And yet, it felt to me as if they had a lot more than we did.

'I thought you wanted a phone,' said Jess, looking over my shoulder at the screen.

'Too expensive,' I replied flatly.

'Mum and Dad pay a pound a week to this company. It doesn't feel expensive when you do it like that, but they get it all back in one chunk at Christmas, and more on top of it. It pays for presents and food and stuff.'

'Mum won't have done anything like that. She thought she'd have another job by now.'

'Well, it's something to think about for next year, isn't it? Look.' Jess clicked on the company's website. It sounded great – that must be how people like us could have a good Christmas.

'I'll mention it to her. Though hopefully, things will be better by next year.'

Jess smiled sadly. 'That's what Dad said when he lost his job. Always thinking there was another one just around the corner. That was nearly five years ago.'

I sighed.

'I'm not saying that will happen to your mum,' Jess added quickly. 'But, you know, things like this are always worth considering – saving for Christmas. Just in case.'

The website was full of colourful photographs of people having a wonderful Christmas – wearing paper hats and ugly jumpers with snowmen on them; sitting in front of tables loaded with turkey and stuffing and vegetables and roast potatoes and cakes and all kinds of other lovely things.

DO YOU KNOW THAT THE AVERAGE FAMILY CHRISTMAS COSTS £856?

The words were written in bold black letters at the top of the screen. 'No way,' I said.

'Just think about it, Meg,' replied Jess. 'Think about all the stuff the kids in our class are having. It costs a fortune. Then all the food and drink. The only time Mum and Dad ever drink wine is at Christmas. And we need chocolates for Gran and bubble bath for Auntie Judith and mince pies in case someone calls … It's endless.'

She was right, of course. Having thought about it, all the little things that make Christmas special also make Christmas expensive. And then I thought about how pale Mum looked, and how thin because she didn't eat as much as she used to, and how whole days went by without her leaving the house. I wondered whether Mum looked forward to Christmas at all, or did she just dread the whole thing?

Sam

It was the best Christmas I'd ever had.

I don't know what happened to Meg, but around the beginning of December she began a new obsession. Over supper one evening, when she'd just returned from the library, she started saying we needed a plan.

'Did you know that the average family Christmas costs £856? £856! It's awful!'

'Well, yes,' agreed Mum, as she ladled soup into three bowls. 'But it's important that we celebrate.'

'Of course. But spending that amount of money isn't celebrating, it's completely stupid. I think we should do things differently this year.'

Fair play to her, Meg was trying to turn saving money into an adventure.

'I don't want you to worry about money too ... ' started Mum.

'I'm not saying it because we're poor, Mum. Well, not just because of that. I really do think it's silly to spend too much on one occasion.'

Neither Mum nor I were convinced by Meg that evening. But slowly, she started to introduce new ideas and small changes. We had plenty of time to make presents for ourselves, she said, if we started thinking about it now. And we didn't have to spend money on new decorations, we could make them ourselves.

One Friday night in mid-December, Mum, Meg and I started to make a Christmassy banner to hang above the fireplace – the plastic 'Merry Christmas' from the year before was tatty and torn. So with an old canvas and old paints, we made a new banner – a huge one, unlike anything you could buy in a shop. It filled up the space above the fireplace, and though it wasn't perfect, it was so much better than last year's. We painted a picture of Mum putting the star on top of the tree, and Meg in a Santa hat, and me with antlers and a red nose like Rudolph. In the centre, we wrote 'Merry Christmas and a Happy New Year!'

'It's time we thought about Christmas lunch,' said Meg a few weeks before the big day. 'I think we should make a list of the food we need. I read online that people spend far too much money on food that gets wasted, or on things they don't really need. The supermarkets use all kinds of tricks to make you buy more, so it's easier if you make a list and stick to it.'

Mum stared open-mouthed at Meg. 'How do you know all this?'

'I went to the library so that I could go on a money-saving website. No, don't look at me like that, Mum. I *wanted* to do it. It's actually very interesting.'

'But what if we make a list, and then go to the supermarket and finds lots of bargains? Are we allowed to buy those, too?' I asked.

Meg shook her head. 'It says on the internet that a true bargain is very rare. For example, if you had a box of chocolates, two for the price of one … '

'Brilliant! Everyone likes chocolate … '

' … but the box is a little bit more expensive than the chocolates we'd usually buy. Well, that's not a bargain at all!'

Mum frowned. 'Of course it is! You get two boxes, but you only have to pay for one … '

'But you only need one, so you've spent extra money on something you might not use!'

I must admit, it took a while for me to understand this. To this day, I'm still drawn to 'buy-one-get-one-free' or 'three-for-the-price-of-two' deals. But Meg was right. Most of them are a complete con.

In the end, the three of us decided on these things:

1) No turkey. Even a small one costs £30, and you can get a stuffed chicken that's almost as big for a fiver.

2) Mum was the only one who liked sprouts, so

we'd only have to buy five or six instead of buying a bag and then throwing most out to the compost.

3) We didn't need more than three kinds of vegetables, so carrots, peas and broccoli were enough. Mum would have sprouts, too, of course. Frozen vegetables were cheaper than fresh.

4) I was the only one who liked Christmas pudding, so we'd buy a tiny one for me and chocolate pudding for Mum and Meg.

5) One box of chocolates was enough, and one packet of mince pies in case anyone popped round. Meg said it would be cheaper to make the mince pies ourselves, but Mum put her foot down on that point and said that she never had got the hang of making pastry.

6) We'd buy big bottles of pop instead of cans, and Mum said she didn't want wine or anything like that as long as she had some cherryade.

In the end, our Christmas food cost £24.82. It was a lot more than we'd usually spend on food, but the chicken lasted for a few days, and it was all very tasty and Christmassy. In a way, it was even better than all the other Christmases, because I didn't have to face the dreaded sprouts.

I know that Mum would have liked to buy Meg and me all the latest gadgets, but she did very well with the money she had. I got lots of adventure books, new pyjamas, and a board game. Meg was given a new dress, make-up and a diary with a lock. But the best things were the presents we'd made for one another. Meg had bought second-hand picture frames and had painted them, and then put photos of us when we were kids in them. Mum had made us our own special plates, and had painted them especially with our names. But my presents were the best. They were vouchers, printed on the computer at the library so that they looked professional.

> # **VOUCHER**
> ## This voucher will get you
> ## **BREAKFAST IN BED**
> ## on a day of your choice.
>
> (Can only be used once. Unavailable on Sundays.)

Mum and Meg loved their vouchers. I'd made lots of different ones – some for breakfast in bed, some for washing the dishes, some to make a sandwich or to pop to the shop. Mum nearly cried when she opened hers.

After we'd had lunch and played my new board game, we settled down to watch a film. When the adverts came on, Mum asked, 'Have you opened your envelopes from Dad yet?'

Meg and I glanced at one another. I'd completely forgotten about the envelopes that had arrived from Dad the week before, plastered with warnings not to be opened before the 25th. I fetched them from under the tree, and passed Meg's over to her.

The card was funny – a cartoon of Santa eating mince pies, cracking someone's roof with his weight. But my smile faded when I opened the card, and saw all the banknotes inside.

Twenties. One, two, three, four, five of them. Five twenties are a hundred. A hundred pounds. I looked over at Meg – she'd had the same.

'That's generous of him,' said Mum gently.

Meg shut the card, and stuffed it all back into the envelope. I did the same, but slower. As we watched the rest of the film, I couldn't help but wonder where Dad was. Was he having a merry Christmas? Was he alone, or did he have someone to keep him company? In my heart, I knew that even though Dad had far more money than us, he wasn't having as nice a Christmas as we were.

Late on Christmas night, we stayed up, watching the lights on the tree. Everything was so pretty, so perfect, and I was happy and sleepy.

'We'd better switch off the fairy lights,' I said, stifling a yawn. 'It's costing a fortune.'

'Not yet,' said Mum, putting her arms around Meg and me. 'Let's keep them on for a just a little while longer.'

Meg

I don't know whether it was a new year's resolution of his, but Dad started phoning us more often in January.

A long time had passed since Mum lost her job, and I'd started to think that our family had changed. Things were still hard – I was still annoyed that I had to go to the library to do my homework instead of having the internet at home like everyone else. Returning to school in January to hear that Jon had been given a horse for Christmas didn't help. But Mum and Sam and I felt like a little family, closer than ever. We were still coping, though we were broke, and that made me feel proud.

I refused to speak to Dad the first few times he called, but the third time, Sam sounded so miserable when he said 'Dad really wants to speak to you', I took the phone from his hand. We were by the kitchen table, eating supper, and Mum was doing her very best not to eavesdrop.

'Hello?'

'Meg! Darling! How are you, chicken?'

My reply stuck in my throat. I'd been ready to say a quick hello just to get rid of him, but hearing his voice felt strange. I'd completely forgotten that he used to call me 'chicken'.

'Okay.'

'You've been very busy recently – you're never around when I phone.' He didn't sound angry, but it was obvious that he knew that I just hadn't wanted to speak to him.

'You didn't phone for months,' I replied, more honest than I'd planned. It would be easier to pretend that I didn't care at all, but somehow I just couldn't, now that his voice was there on the phone. 'I'm used to coping without you.'

'Sorry, chicken,' said Dad, his voice barely more than a whisper. 'I am, really, I am. It wasn't right. Please, Meggy, give me another chance.'

I couldn't answer that. What exactly did he mean? Did he want another chance to live with us? Or was chatting every now and then on the phone enough for him?

'Think about it, Meg. Sam can forgive. And I'd love to see you both.'

'Okay.'

'Okay?'

'Okay, I'll think about it, not okay, I'll see you.'

I heard Dad sighing softly, then he said, 'All right, chicken. Whatever you want.'

I couldn't sleep that night. Hearing Dad's voice had unsettled me. Even after everything, I couldn't hate him. He had sounded the same as he always had; the same as when he used to come into our bedroom at night to read us a story. And yet, I was so angry with him. I didn't need him any more, and he hadn't been there when Mum lost her job. He didn't offer help. Who did he think he was, thinking he could come and go as he pleased?

Your father, that's who he is, said a little voice in my head. I fell asleep slowly, unable to decide whether I was furious or glad that I'd heard my dad's voice for the first time in months.

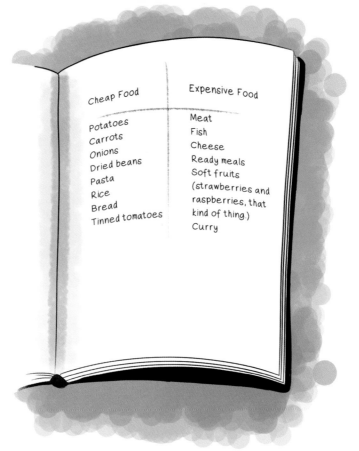

Cheap Food	Expensive Food
Potatoes	Meat
Carrots	Fish
Onions	Cheese
Dried beans	Ready meals
Pasta	Soft fruits
Rice	(strawberries and
Bread	raspberries, that
Tinned tomatoes	kind of thing.)
	Curry

Sam

Beans.

I was fed up of them.

I don't mean baked beans, that kind you get in a tin with loads of orange sauce. I love baked beans – I could live on those. But Mum had found a cheap, healthy recipe, and though I'd quite liked it at the beginning of autumn, by the end of January, I was desperate for something different.

'Bean stew again?' said Meg one evening. She was

in a bad mood anyway - Dad had phoned, and that always put her in a bad temper.

'It's good for you. And it's cheap,' Mum replied.

'But I want something different for a change.'

'Okay, then,' said Mum, finally losing her patience. 'You cook something healthy that costs the same, Meg.' Meg shut up then. She hated cooking.

But I started thinking that I might like to have a go. Not that I was any good at cooking, but it sounded like a challenge. So after supper I spoke to Mum.

'How much does it cost to make bean stew?'

'I'm not sure. But it isn't a lot. I buy big bags of dried beans, and soak them overnight. That's a lot cheaper than buying them in tins.'

Though it wasn't easy to work out how much everything cost, it was something like this:

Onion	15p
Carrot	20p
Stock cube	32p
Beans	35p
Peas	35p
	137p = £1.37

Goodness. That was a hearty meal for the three of us – I always felt full after bean stew. And £1.37 divided by three was ... Well, it was a difficult sum, and I had to borrow the calculator on Mum's phone. After I had the answer, I gazed up at Mum in admiration.

'You're really clever, Mum.'

She chuckled in surprise. 'Am I? My teachers at school never mentioned it ... '

'You really are. Bean stew costs us about 46p each. 46p! That's less than a bar of chocolate!'

Mum grinned. 'Well, I'm glad you appreciate it. Meg isn't keen on bean stew.'

I didn't like to admit that I was fed up of it, too, even if it was a bargain. 'Mum? Can I try to cook?'

Mum looked doubtful. 'Sam, it's not fun having to buy the very cheapest things all the time ... '

'But I'll enjoy it! Please, Mum. We can go to the shop after school tomorrow. I won't spend any more than you, and I'll do the cooking. You'll only have to help me with the oven and the hob ... Please!

And so, the very next day, I had the chance to wander around the supermarket.

Do you know, it's surprising what food is cheap and what food is expensive. I made a list in my notebook.

Cheap Food	Expensive Food
Potatoes	Meat
Carrots	Fish
Onions	Cheese
Dried beans	Ready meals
Pasta	Soft fruits
Rice	(strawberries and
Bread	raspberries, that
Tinned tomatoes	kind of thing.)
	Curry

So, after making a few quick sums in my notebook, I chose a few things for Mum's basket, starting to feel a bit nervous about cooking for the family.

Fair play to Mum. She was brilliant at helping me, for taking things out of the oven when they were hot and standing over me while I stirred something in a saucepan, making sure nothing was burnt. And do you know what? It was fun. If I had been able to go to the supermarket to choose whatever I wanted, I would have picked a huge pizza or a ready-made curry. But there was no challenge in cooking things like that - that's why they were so cheap.

Over the next few weeks, I cooked:

Pasta and tomato sauce with onions and peas

Pasta	30p
Tomato sauce	57p
Onion	20p
Peas	35p
	142p = £1.42

£1.42 divided by 3, is around 47p each.

<u>Tomato and rice soup</u>

Tomato sauce	5 7 p
Onion	2 0 p
Rice	2 5 p
	1 0 2 p = £ 1 . 0 2

£1.02 divided by 3, is 34p each.

<u>Pasta with bean puree</u>

Pasta	3 0 p
Beans	3 5 p
Garlic	3 0 p
Onion	2 0 p
	1 1 5 p = £ 1 . 1 5

£1.15 divided by 3, is around 38p each.

That last one was by far the best. I'd noticed how cheap it was to buy garlic in a tube – not the fresh sort that was a pain to peel and chop. For a while, I put it in everything, until Meg told me to go easy because we were all starting to stink.

Around the same time, Meg and I started having school dinners.

Years ago, Mum had said that she preferred it if we had a packed lunch – something to do with knowing exactly what we ate. But now, because Mum had lost her job, we could have school dinners for free.

Mum seemed nervous when she told us. One morning, over breakfast, she said, 'I spoke to Miss Evans yesterday.'

Miss Evans works in the office at school. She's sweet and kind, and everyone loves her. Still, I was surprised that Mum spoke to her. Had something happened at school?

'I've decided that you should have school dinners. We don't have to pay, and it means that you'd get a good meal there.'

'Okay,' said Meg, searching her bag for a book she'd lost. 'Oh, rats! I've lost my spelling book again … Have you seen it? I'm sure I had it yesterday … '

'You don't mind?' Mum asked, surprised.

'Ha! I've been wanting to try that chocolate cake they have for pudding on Wednesdays for donkey's years,' replied Meg. She waved her battered spelling book triumphantly. 'Oh, I've found it! Phew.'

'Goodness!' Mum exclaimed, covering her eyes with her hands. 'I've been worried that you'd get upset …'

I shook my head. 'Are we starting today? They have spaghetti bolognaise on Tuesdays … It smells amazing … ' I took a deep breath, as if I could smell it in our kitchen.

'Next week,' Mum smiled. 'And thank you, both of you.'

'What for?' asked Meg as she pulled on her coat.

'For not complaining.'

One day, by the tills in the supermarket, Mum wrapped her arms around me. I pulled back, worried that someone from school would see.

'What are you doing?' I asked.

'Didn't you notice, sweetheart? Porridge for breakfast, a free lunch and your cheap recipes for supper – we just bought a whole week's shopping for £10 exactly.'

I'd never felt so proud.

Meg

Dad came to see us.

I knew he would, sooner or later, once he'd started phoning us. Nan was phoning a lot, too, but only to boast how wonderful her amazing son was. I would put the call on speakerphone and would put it on the table, doing my homework as she went on and on.

'And your father has the most wonderful flat in Cardiff Bay. Well! You can see across the water to the Welsh Assembly, and all the yachts coming and going. And he's doing so well in his new job, and he goes to the gym twice a week now … ' As long as I said the occasional 'mmhm,' or 'Oh, that's nice', Nan could speak for hours. I wrote pages and pages of homework, did tens of sums, read whole books while I was on the phone with Nan. Sometimes Mum would be in the kitchen too, trying to make me pay attention to what Nan was saying. But she had to leave, once, because she laughed so much when Nan said,

'I do enjoy our conversations on the phone, Meg. I feel like I know you so much better after hearing about your life.' I never said a word about my life – I never had the chance. She filled up the whole time talking about Dad.

Anyway, it was arranged that Dad would come and see us one Saturday. He and Mum had been talking, and Sam and I weren't given a choice. Mum just told us on Friday evening, 'Your Dad is coming here tomorrow, and he'll be taking you out for lunch.' I started saying something along the lines of 'Over my dead body', but Mum didn't give me a chance. 'Don't start, Meg. It's only lunch. I'm expecting you both to be polite.'

'It wasn't very polite of him to take off like that and not get in touch for months,' I replied frostily.

'I know it's not easy for you. But I can't answer questions for your dad. You need to speak to him yourselves.'

'Are you coming?' Sam asked Mum.

'No.'

'I'd prefer it if you came.'

'It's only fair that Dad gets time alone with you. That's the right thing to do.'

Sam sighed. I was surprised that he didn't seem keen to go for lunch with Dad – he was always so happy to speak to him on the phone.

'Go out, enjoy your lunch, and be kind to your father,' said Mum with a weak little smile.

'But I don't *feel* like being kind to him,' I tried to explain.

'I know, sweetheart. But Dad is coming to see you. He's trying, and that's the most important thing.'

Nan was right. Dad *did* look good.

He stepped out of his posh car and grinned when he saw us standing in the window. He wore neat jeans and a white shirt, and his black hair glinted with gel. I'd forgotten how handsome he was, like a film star. One of the strangest things was, he looked really odd here, though he'd lived here for years.

When we opened the door, Dad held Sam and me close. He still smelled the same – expensive aftershave. I'd forgotten that smell.

'You're so big!' he said after he finally let go of us. His big eyes shone as if he was about to cry. 'I can't believe how tall you are!'

'People change a lot in nine months,' I replied, because that's how long it had been since he'd seen us and I wanted to remind him of that.

'Of course,' Dad nodded sadly. He looked up, and saw Mum standing in the kitchen behind us. 'Hi, Karen.'

'Hello.' Mum smiled, and I wanted to yell at her. *Don't smile at him! He doesn't deserve your smile!* But I stayed silent.

'Goodness! It's cold in here!' said Dad. 'Right, are

you two ready to go?'

'Central heating is very expensive you know, Dad,' said Sam innocently.

Dad nodded and Mum blushed.

The restaurant was about half an hour away, and was very, very posh. There were huge windows with a view across the river and down to the estuary. There were no other children there – in fact, it reminded me of the place Nan had taken us in Aberystwyth. I didn't look at the menu properly – I'd already decided that I was having the most expensive thing on the menu, whatever it was.

'Are you sure you like oysters?' Dad asked after we'd ordered the first course. 'Do you know what they are? Little slimy things in shells … ' They sounded horrible, but they cost £8, so I just nodded.

When the oysters came to the table, they looked as if someone had sneezed into shells. Sam stared at them as he ate his chicken salad, and Dad watched me as he sipped his soup.

'You put the shell to your mouth and tip your head back, letting it slip down your throat. You're not meant to chew oysters, just swallow them as they are.'

The smell was enough to make me want to puke. But I had no choice – I had ordered them. So I swallowed the disgusting oyster.

I refused to even look at any more.

Dad was annoyed with me, I could tell, though he did his best to hide it. To be honest, I deserved a good telling-off, because I went out of my way to be as irritating and awkward as I could that afternoon. I ordered a huge steak for my main course, because it was the most expensive thing they had, and then took forty five minutes to chew the meat. Dad stared at me, as if he was trying to solve a tricky problem, but he didn't dare say anything. I think he knew that I was ready for an argument if only he'd give me an excuse to yell at him.

I didn't say much over lunch, but Sam chatted as if Dad hadn't done anything wrong at all. I was angry at him for forgiving so easily. That was the trouble with Sam – he wanted to please everybody.

Over dessert (cheesecake – the only part of the meal I actually enjoyed), I decided to switch tactics. Instead of staying silent, I started to talk. I talked over dessert, as Dad paid the bill, in the car, and as we went for a walk by the river. I only had one subject. Mum.

The plan was that speaking about how wonderful Mum had been this last year would make Dad feel bad about not being there at all.

'Mum reads with us for an hour every evening. Miss Edwards says that it's the reason Sam and I are so good at spelling – it's all because of Mum.'

'Fair play to Mum, she never moans that she can't go out these days. Babysitters are so expensive! How about you, Dad? I bet you go out all the time.'

And my personal favourite: 'Mum's been incredible. She's been a mother and a father to Sam and me these last months.'

There was a long silence after that. I felt great, because I was sure Dad felt awful.

'I'm not stupid, Meg. I know I haven't been there for you recently. And I'm sorry.' His voice was quiet, and yes, he did sound as if he felt guilty. But I didn't care. He deserved to know the mess he left when he went away.

I was about to open my mouth and tell him, when Dad piped up, 'I'm here now, and I don't want to be without you again. I'm going to try to make it right.'

'Huh,' I mumbled. I looked over at Sam – he was walking silently, his hands buried deep in his coat pockets, staring at his shoes. He looked totally miserable.

'I thought it'd be nice if you came to stay with me on the weekend before your birthday. You'll like my flat – it's in Cardiff Bay – and we'll go out for dinner. Your birthday is on the Wednesday, so you'll still be with your mum on the day itself.'

Our birthday. I hadn't thought about it much since we decided not to go to Oak Park. There were only about six weeks to go. Mum had mentioned having a pizza and one or two guests – nothing big, though we all hoped there'd be more money to celebrate next year.

'And on the Saturday, I thought we might go to Oak Park,' added Dad. 'It's not too far from Cardiff, and I've always wanted to go.'

Sam

Meg tried to say no.

No. It was more than that. She had a real tantrum, stamping through the house in a temper, yelling at Dad on the phone. 'Cardiff, okay, only for a weekend. But I won't go to Oak Park with you. I WON'T.'

Living with her was hell, and I started doing something that had become a bit of a habit: I fetched my little notebook and did a few sums.

Before it all happened, before Dad left and before

Mum lost her job, I used to hate doing maths at school. I preferred to write a story or draw a picture. But something about doing these kinds of sums made sense to me – I was working out real things, adding up money or figuring out how much we were saving. Seeing the numbers written down neatly made everything easier for me, as if I could work anything out.

So when Meg yelled down the phone at Dad, 'I don't want to see you!', I worked out how much tickets to Oak Park could cost. And when Mum tried to reason with her: 'He's still your father, whether you like him or not', I was trying to figure out the value of Dad's posh car. And when I was in the bottom bunk and Meg was in the top, pretending that she was sniffing because of a cold and not because she was crying, I was trying to work out the difference in rent between our small house and a posh flat in Cardiff Bay.

We had to go to Dad's in the end, of course. I don't know what Mum said to Meg, but they had a long chat over a tub of ice cream one evening, and Meg seemed less angry after that.

Dad came to get us in his car. I looked through the back window, waving at Mum until we rounded the corner. I wasn't worried about her – she'd planned her whole weekend, going for a long walk and then a meal with one of her old school friends. But it was still odd without her. It had been a long time since we'd spent a night apart, and it made me feel like a little boy.

In two hours, the car had sped its way towards the city and was crawling through the traffic on the outskirts. I'd never been in such a posh car. The seats were made of soft leather, and the stereo made it sound as if Elvis was actually in the car with us and not warbling through the mp3 player.

'I'm so glad you'll be seeing my home,' Dad grinned. 'I hope you'll want to stay with me often.'

'Nan has been telling us about the flat,' I said from the back seat.

'Not just the flat – the whole city. There's so much to do there. Museums, theatres, cinemas … '

'There's a cinema in our town,' Meg said flatly. 'We live in the countryside, not the dark ages.'

I was expecting Dad to be annoyed, but he laughed as if Meg had told a wonderful joke. After I while, I started laughing, too, and though I suspected that Meg had decided to be as awkward as possible before she came, she, too, started giggling.

Dad said that we'd been to Cardiff before, when we were little, but I couldn't remember. I had never seen such a busy place – cars and shops and houses and people. Dad drove from one side of the city to the other, pointing things out as he drove – 'That's where the big shops are'; 'That Indian restaurant on the corner is the best in the city'; 'Can you see the Millennium Stadium over there? That's where they have all the big rugby matches.'

At last, Dad stopped the car in a huge car park by a lot of flats. The buildings were massive, and looked brand new. After fetching our bags from the boot of the car, we went into one of the buildings, and stepped into the lift.

'Which floor?' asked Meg before pressing the button.

'Nine.'

'Nine?' repeated Meg in surprise.

Dad smiled widely. 'The higher you go, the better

the views.'

I have to admit, I hadn't expected Dad's flat to be like it was. Though Nan had gone on about how posh it was, I'd still imagined that it would be somehow similar to our house. After all, that's where he'd lived until last year. But the flat was amazing.

Shining black floors; a gleaming metal kitchen; and the windows! Reaching from the floors to the ceilings, with a lovely view across the bay.

Dad chuckled as he saw the expressions on our faces. 'You like it, then?'

'It's like somewhere from an advert,' I answered slowly. 'I didn't think people really lived in places like this … '

'I'm very lucky,' Dad said. 'This new job of mine … Now! Let me show you to your room.'

There was only one single bed in the bedroom, but Dad had put an airbed on the floor. It was a small room, and dark, but I didn't mind.

'You take the bed,' said Meg.

'Are you sure?'

'Yes. You're the one who has trouble sleeping, not me.' I was glad. Though I felt okay, I thought I might have trouble when it came to sleeping, being so far away from Mum and home.

It's strange how quickly you can get used to something. For an hour or two, Dad's house felt like a hotel, and Meg and I weren't sure what to do. It was like being in a stranger's house. Though we were thirsty, we didn't ask for a drink but waited for Dad to offer, and we didn't put on the huge 60-inch telly, but waited for Dad to put it on for us.

After I asked if I could go to the toilet, Dad said, 'You're both to treat this flat like home. You don't have to ask to use the toilet, you can watch the telly or play on the computer whenever you want.' He took us to the kitchen and showed us where he kept the pop, and said we could help ourselves. He had the purple pop I like, and when I saw it, Dad turned to me and said, 'I remember that it's your favourite, Sam.'

After that, Meg and I made ourselves at home. In no time at all, we were arguing about which channel to watch, and gulping pop straight from the bottle. Dad ordered us a pizza each, and within half an hour a man had brought them to the door. Dad wasn't given much change from three ten pound notes, but I still enjoyed the food.

Do you know the strangest thing? Meg. I think we'd all expected her to battle with Dad – she'd been going on and on about how much she wanted to stay at home, and that she couldn't care less about Cardiff. But by the time we'd filled our bellies with pizza and sat back on the leather sofa to watch a film, she was perfectly happy, laughing and joking with him. And, when I got up halfway through the meal to get a drink, I noticed that Meg – angry, independent Meg – had fallen asleep with her head on Dad's shoulder.

That's when it started.

I'd never felt anything like it before. It was a quaking deep in my stomach. I started to think I'd eaten too much, but no – this was something else. I lay in bed after the film, not feeling in the least bit sleepy. The muscles in my arms and legs felt full of energy, and I felt like running, like getting up and racing downstairs and sprinting around this huge city.

I got up at midnight to use the bathroom, and Dad got up when he heard me. 'Can't sleep, Sammy? You can leave the landing light on all night if it makes you feel better.'

'No thanks. It uses too much electricity. I'd rather turn out the light.'

I couldn't explain it to myself at the time – it was a new feeling. But by the time I awoke the next morning, it had grown instead of getting smaller, and all day – in the car, in Oak Park, in the fast-food restaurant, on the way back to Cardiff – the feeling grew and grew until I thought I might burst.

Meg

I won't go on about how amazing Oak Park was. You've probably heard it a thousand times before - seen the adverts, or heard people saying that the rides are brilliant. But it *was* amazing. I had a wonderful day.

Dad was amazing, too.

Before we went to Cardiff, I'd decided never to forgive him. The only reason I agreed to go at all was because it would give me the chance to irritate Dad. I'd be as awkward as possible, and complain about everything, and make his life hell for the whole weekend.

But the truth is, though I was still angry, I loved Dad. I don't think anything could have changed that. I wasn't ready yet to forgive the months and months that had gone by without a single phone call from him. I wasn't going to discuss that now – I didn't feel ready. This was the time to remember the good things about one another, and to enjoy each other's company.

Sam didn't seem quite right in Oak Park – I don't think he'd slept very well the night before. He was quiet in the car, and he wasn't as keen as Dad and me to go on the rides. As we queued for rides, he spent all his time scribbling in his little notebook.

'Is he okay, d'you think?' Dad asked as he and I took our seats on *Fear Drop 3.0*. Sam was sitting on a bench, waiting for us.

'I don't know. He's quieter than usual. Maybe he's worried about Mum – he's always worrying about something.'

'What's that little book? A diary?'

I shook my head. 'Lists. Sums, usually.'

'What, homework?'

'No. Things like working out how much it costs to make a certain meal. How much we spend per week. That kind of thing.'

Dad frowned. 'That sounds like a weird hobby for a boy his age. He never liked maths when I ... ' He wasn't brave enough to finish the sentence – *when I lived with you*.

'It started when Mum lost her job. He was trying to help us to spend a bit less. But Miss Edwards says his maths has improved a lot at school ... he's one of the best in our class now.'

Then the roller coaster started moving, and before we knew it, Dad and I were screaming with pleasure and fear, being thrown upside down and side to side. It was great, and Dad held my hand throughout everything.

On the ground, Sam sat on the bench, alone amongst all the people.

Dad wasn't like Nan. When we went shopping in Oak Park, he raised one eyebrow when I tried to convince him to buy me a £40 necklace.

'I wasn't born yesterday, Meg. You can spend £10 each, and no more.'

I spent my money on a photograph of the three of us. It had been taken when we were on one of the water rides and just about to plummet down and get soaked. Dad and I were screaming but smiling, and I realised how similar we were – dark hair and light skin, the same smile. Sam sat in the seat behind us, with a pained look on his face. I couldn't help but laugh when I first saw the photo – Sam was such a worrier, and you could see that in the picture.

Sam bought only a biro in the shop, though Dad tried to convince him to spend more. 'You can afford a new notebook, too, Sam – I'm sure that one you have is filling up.'

'No thanks,' Sam replied politely. 'But I really like the biro. Thank you.'

On the way back to Cardiff, we stopped at a fast-food restaurant. You know the kind of place - plastic tables, different kinds of burgers and sauces, and teenagers wearing red hats taking the orders. Although we'd had a big lunch, I was starving.

'Well, that was one of the best days I've had in ages,' Dad said after he'd eaten half of his burger. 'But I don't think I can finish my food. All that spinning on rides has given me a funny tummy.'

'I'll finish it, when I've eaten mine,' I answered through a mouthful of meat. 'Woooow, this burger is lovely!'

'So is mine. Thank you, Dad,' Sam agreed politely.

Dad was quiet for a while, and then he said, 'It's okay, Sam. You don't have to thank me for everything. I'm your father – it's my job to look after you.'

I hadn't noticed until he said that, but having thought about it, Sam had said thank you for every single thing all weekend. Thank you for the welcome; thank you for letting us watch telly; thank you for feeding us. He sounded like someone who was staying at the home of a stranger.

'Sorry,' Sam said weakly.

Dad smiled. 'You don't need to apologise. But really. It's a pleasure having you with me, and I like looking after you. Now, when Meg's finished stuffing her face – who wants dessert?'

And though Sam smiled and chose a dessert, I noticed that he was doing something that I'd never seen him doing before. His fist was closed so tightly that the knuckles had gone all white.

Something was wrong.

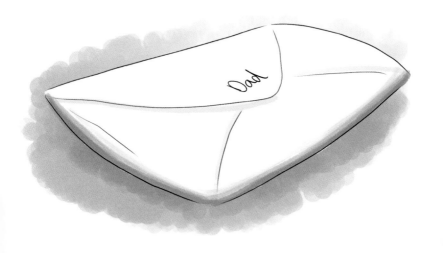

Sam

Sunday morning. I'd packed my things before Dad and Meg woke up, and I sat on the sofa watching cartoons with the volume turned down low until Meg joined me. Dad soon joined us, grinning happily, his hair still wet after a shower.

'Good morning, chickens! Did you sleep?'

'Yeah,' replied Meg.

'Yes,' I replied, though I'd barely slept at all.

'Great! I thought we'd go for breakfast to one of

the cafes down the road – there's one that does amazing pancakes. To fill you up before you go home. What do you think?'

'Sounds good,' said Meg, yawning. 'I can't believe it's time to go home already!'

'Me neither.' Dad switched on the coffee machine. 'It's feels like you've only just arrived. But I hope you'll come back again soon. I haven't showed you the city, and I'd like you to meet my friends and see where I work … '

A programme about horses started on telly, and I fetched my notebook. It was a terrible programme, but Meg loved it.

'Still scribbling, Sam?' asked Dad. 'Are you going to show me these sums, then?'

It was then that I realised what it was, that shivering feeling in my tummy that had been growing and growing all weekend. The hardening of my muscles, my fist becoming tight. I hadn't realised before, because I'd never felt that emotion before – at least, nowhere near this much.

I was angry.

No, not angry. Furious. Raging. For the first time ever, I felt like screaming and swearing.

It wasn't a pleasant feeling. I didn't know whether I could trust what I was about to say. My words felt dangerous.

'They don't mean anything to anyone else,' I said quietly, starting to sweat.

'But I'd still like to see them,' Dad insisted. 'Come and sit at the table with me. Show me.'

I felt as if I was dreaming as I walked over to the table. I sat by Dad, and opened the first page.

'This is a list of what used to go into our lunch boxes,' I explained quietly. 'We had to cut back after Mum lost her job. So this was our lunch boxes afterwards.' I pointed to the second list. 'Less tasty and not so interesting, but we saved £16.30 a week!'

I saw Dad swallowing hard as he stared at the list. I don't think he'd realized before that point how poor we were. 'Very clever, Sam. It's brilliant that you managed to work that out.'

'We get free school dinners now,' called Meg from the sofa. Half her attention was on us, and half was on the telly. 'It's great.'

I turned the page. 'This is how much a picnic cost us when we went for a long walk in the hills. I like this one, because it proves that you don't have to spend money to have a good time.'

Dad nodded. He didn't know what to say.

'I did these sums after Nan took us out for the day. That's how much my lunch cost – the price of my lunch box for a whole month! This is how much Nan spent on clothes for us – can you see?' I showed the numbers to Dad.

'That's kind of Nan,' said Dad quietly. 'She enjoyed that day with you.'

'She was very very rude to Mum,' I answered. 'If I was a braver person, I would have told her to mind her manners.'

Dad stared at me, his mouth hanging open. Meg turned slowly, her eyes wide. It wasn't like me to be so prickly.

'Sam!' Meg exclaimed.

'She said that taking us out for the day would give Mum a chance to clean.' I turned to Meg. 'Didn't she,

Meg?'

'Well, yes, but that's what Nan is like ... '

'That's no excuse.'

I turned the pages of the notebook. 'This is the Christmas list of what I wanted. It would have cost £342.98. This one is the list that Mum saw – £28.50. And this is the sum Meg and I worked out together to save money on Christmas dinner – chicken instead of turkey, no wine for Mum. She pretended that she didn't want any. That was nice of her, wasn't it?'

My voice was hard now, nothing like the voice that had been saying 'thank you' for every little thing from him. I felt strange, as if it was someone else was saying these words.

'But Dad gave us a hundred pounds each for Christmas,' said Meg weakly. She had switched off the television and had come to sit with us.

'Yes. Thank you for that, Dad. It felt odd, having more money than Mum.'

Dad wiped his forehead with the back of his hand. 'I didn't know ... '

'These are the sums I did about two months ago, trying to find out a way we could go to Oak Park with Mum on our birthday, as we'd planned months and months ago. But we had to choose between putting on the central heating and going to Oak Park, and we picked the heating.' I looked around the luxurious flat. 'By the way, it's lovely and warm in here, Dad.'

I don't remember a lot after that. It's as if my memory has deleted the worst bits. But after we went home, after we'd seen Mum again and slept in our own beds for a few nights, Meg went over it with Mum and me.

' ... And Sam said that it was hard to enjoy the posh flat and the expensive car when we lived on practically nothing!'

'You never said that!' Mum turned to me.

'I can't really remember,' I admitted. 'I was so angry, Mum.'

'And then he said that even though the flat was worth a fortune, it would never be a home, and please could Dad hurry up with breakfast so that we could go home as soon as possible.'

'I can't believe it,' said Mum. 'It doesn't sound like my little Sam!'

'That's not even the best bit! Then, Sam stood up and said in a low voice, "Maybe Mum doesn't have a lot of money, but having her as a mother makes me feel rich".'

Mum started crying, and Meg looked at me with real admiration, as if I'd done something truly brave.

And perhaps I had. Not that losing my temper with Dad did any good – it would probably have been better to explain my feelings when I wasn't so angry. But my notebook of sums had made a difference to me. It wasn't just lists and sums, but whole stories, and the tale of what happened to our family when things started to go wrong.

There were some sums that even Meg and Mum weren't allowed to see.

You see, Miss Edwards had just started to teach us about percentages. We hadn't got very far with them, but I understood enough to leave my Christmas money in an envelope on Dad's kitchen table, and wrote neatly on it:

Mum spends £10 a week on food for the three of us. £10 is 10% of £100. It is too much. Please send this money to Mum. She won't take it from me.

Meg

There's no such thing as a happy ending.

Well, not completely happy, anyway. Real life isn't like that. Sometimes, things are great, and sometimes they aren't. That's life.

But things got better for us.

The first thing was our birthday. Just Sam and me, Mum, Oli and Jess making pizzas at home, and then scoffing them as we watched a DVD that we'd borrowed from the library. The kitchen looked awful, as if there'd been a flour explosion. The pizzas were delicious, almost as good as the ones we had in Cardiff with Dad. Of course, Sam worked out how much it cost us to have pizza and birthday cake – it was about £3 a head, which was more than we usually spent, but still good value.

On the morning of our birthday, the postman bought a package each for us, both with a Cardiff postmark. For me, a beautiful butterfly necklace, and for Sam, a nice hard-backed notebook and a set of pens. We had a card each, and this is what Dad wrote in Sam's card:

To Sam on your birthday,
Here is a new notebook in case the other one gets full. I'm proud of you and your sums – you've taught me a lot. Never stop working things out.
Lots of love, Dad.

He phoned us every other night, and Sam and I went to stay with him for the weekend about once a month. It wasn't a lot, but it was something, and Sam didn't seem angry with him anymore.

Once, when Dad bought us back from Cardiff, he asked for five minutes' privacy so that he could speak to Mum. I thought he was going to ask her whether they could get back together. Sometimes, late at night, I thought how lovely it would be if he came back, having Mum and Dad together again, the four of us in the same house. After Dad said goodbye to us all and drove away, I asked Mum, 'Are you getting back together?'

Mum burst out laughing, and shook her head. 'You might as well stop thinking about that right now, Meg. It isn't going to happen.'

'What did he want, then?'

'It was a private conversation. It's none of your business.'

But I think they were discussing money, because things were easier for us after that. Not easy, mind you, but not quite as difficult. And you can never really forget, if you've ever been poor. Sam and I never forgot to turn out the light at night.

In no time at all, it was time for Jon's birthday party again. I couldn't believe that a whole year had passed since that ridiculous evening with the fireworks and the volcano cake.

True to form, Jon's parents went overboard again. Somehow, they managed to get a small fairground to come to town, five or six small rides in a field on the edge of town, with toffee apples and a candy floss machine. Jess fell on the whirligig and split her lip. Exactly like last year, I thought it was an awful party, and Sam thought it was fabulous.

Back at home. Mum was curled up on the sofa with a book. She set down the book as we came in. 'Tell me everything,' she said.

'It was terrible,' I replied, kicking off my shoes.

'It was incredible,' said Sam, shrugging off his coat.

'I've got some news,' said Mum. 'The woman who got the job in the Teapot is moving away. They've just phoned to offer me the job.' Sam and I stared at Mum, our mouths gaping. 'I start on Monday.'

So there it is – the story of when our mum lost her job. I could tell you a lot more, like when Sam won the school maths prize, and when Dad moved a bit closer to our town, and when Nan sent Mum a huge bunch of flowers to apologise if she'd ever said anything hurtful. But that's a different story.

Sam

A cup of tea and 2 slices of toast - breakfast in bed for Mum - about 8p

A postcard and stamp to tell Dad I'm thinking of him - 76p

A quick phone call to Nan - about 50p

A surprise bar of chocolate for Meg - 60p

= I feel rich, now.

Money
Matters

Also in the series

978-1-78390-069-5

978-1-78390-070-1

978-1-78390-071-8

In addition to the novels, the series has a designated website for readers that includes interactive activities which provide further opportunities for readers to consider the financial situations that occur within the text.

For more information, go to
www.canolfanpeniarth.org/moneymatters